DANGER BOY

City of Ruins

Mark London Williams

CANDLEWICK PRESS
CAMBRIDGE, MASSACHUSETTS

First edition 2007

Library of Congress Cataloging-in-Publication Data
Williams, Mark London.
City of ruins / Mark London Williams. —1st ed.
p.   cm. — (Danger boy)
Summary: Having traced a dimensional rift to Jerusalem in 583 B.C.E.,
DARPA sends thirteen-year-old Eli and his friends into the past to try to
prevent the unraveling of history and the spread of the deadly slow pox.
ISBN 978-0-7636-2871-0
[1. Time travel — Fiction. 2. Science fiction.]   I. Title.
PZ7.W66697Cit   2007
[Fic] — dc22   2006049076

10 9 8 7 6 5 4 3 2 1

Printed in the United States of America

This book was typeset in Slimbach Book.

Candlewick Press
2067 Massachusetts Avenue
Cambridge, Massachusetts 02140

visit us at www.candlewick.com

This one's for those who came before,
especially the grandfolks:
Don and Cathryn, Lil and Lionel

Prologue

"I wish I could be eight forever...."

The boy keeps throwing rocks against the ruins of the palace wall, trying to hit the outline of a man he's drawn there. The sketch looks like it was done with ash or charcoal. "If I could stay eight, then maybe no more bad things could happen ever again. Or if I could go back to being seven, that would be better—that was before all the bad things happened. But no one can go backward in time."

The rock hits the charcoal man in the head. "There. That's for the soldier who took my parents."

Another rock hits the chalk soldier in the face.

The boy remembers all the screams—remembers the men with their spears and swords and metal helmets, coming and slashing their way through his city,

Jerusalem. Killing the people and the animals, then setting fire to everything that was left.

The idea wasn't to capture the city, but to destroy it.

The boy was small enough to hide in an empty clay jug that stood on the floor of his house, a jug used for storing olive oil.

His bigger sister wasn't so lucky. She didn't find a hiding place in time.

When one of the soldiers kicked the jug over and watched it roll away before setting fire to his family's house, the boy was careful not to scream, the way his parents had warned him not to.

But he couldn't help hearing their screams—and his sister's—as they were taken away.

Not everyone was killed—many were taken to be slaves, slaves for the conquering king, who, like all kings, was looking for ways to make his empire grow.

And those not killed or captured were simply left behind—the old and broken, or, like the boy, the very young—left behind to fend for themselves in a ruined city, with no food, no markets, and no buildings, and each day growing colder, as fall turned into winter.

There weren't even any outside walls left, to clearly define where the city had been.

But the walls had been for keeping invaders out, and they had failed, so what was their point?

Who would want to invade a city of ruins?

Who would even want to visit it?

That's why this new visitor, this older boy, this young man, is so strange to the first boy, throwing his rocks.

He would seem stranger still if the first boy knew that he was a time traveler.

The time traveler watches the boy, his lingo-spot tingling, letting him understand the boy's words in his own tongue.

And with understanding comes a soft, sad smile. He doesn't tell the boy that as it turns out, you can go backward in time. The thing you can't do is stay eight forever.

The time traveler remembers when he was younger, when he threw rocks, when maybe he wished he could be eight or nine or ten forever. There were no ruined cities around him then, back in New Jersey, back in Herronton Woods, running home to a house he thought he might live in forever, with a family he didn't think could ever come apart. He'd run, pretending to be a Barnstormers character—a monster from his favorite Comnet game—playing with his friend Andy. Andy.

Anderson Wall.

He hasn't seen Andy or heard from him, in . . . months? Years? Or really, now that he's become unstuck in time, become "Danger Boy," maybe centuries. It certainly feels like centuries.

"What's your name?" *the first boy asks, still throwing rocks at the soldier on the wall. And though the burnt-orange rays from the setting sun make the boy squint, his aim is steady.*

"Eli."

"Isn't that the name of a priest? Were you a priest at the temple?"

Eli shakes his head. He can understand the boy but knows the boy won't be able to understand his English. "No."

"Are you one of those prophets?"

"No." *Another shake.*

"Then why would you come here? Did they leave you behind, too? Did you hide? Did you escape?"

Eli just shrugs and works on making his smile as sympathetic as possible. The boy keeps talking.

"I mean from the soldiers. The Babylonians. They took everyone they wanted, to make them slaves. Like my mother and father. My sister, too. There must be some reason they left you."

Thunk. Another rock grazes the soldier's arm.

Eli shrugs again—he wishes he could talk to the boy, but he can't risk sharing any of the lingo-spot, since the side effects of the substance are becoming increasingly unpredictable. Instead, he looks around for a stone.

Thunk. This time the boy hits the soldier right in the head. The sun has shifted lower and the light has become redder, so that the ruined wall and the charcoal invader look like they're covered in blood.

Eli holds up his own stone, letting the boy know he'd like a turn.

Now it's the boy's turn to shrug, trying too hard to show he's beyond caring about anything now.

Eli looks at the boy, then stares hard at the wall,

telling himself that the charcoal man isn't a soldier but a catcher, waiting for a pitch. He winds up, shakes off a signal, shakes off another one, then nods—and throws.

"Strike!"

A swamp zombie just swung at a third strike, for the final out of the inning.

"You're outta there!" Eli jerks his thumb, remembering how much fun it was when the monsters were easy to beat, but he doesn't realize how loud he's yelling, and the boy jumps back.

"Hey!" The boy clutches another rock in his hand, and it looks like he might throw this one at Eli.

Eli holds out his hands and tries to explain. "I'm playing Barnstormers."

"I still don't understand you," the boy says. "Where are you really from? Why did you come here?"

Eli can see the boy is shaking now, trembling all over, trying to be brave but on the verge of tears. Eli steps closer. "It's all right."

"I can't understand you!"

"I'm not here to hurt you."

"Just stay away."

"I know what you're feeling. I do." Another step.

"I mean it."

And closer still, as the red sun falls farther below the horizon and the bloody light turns to shadow. Then Eli is next to the boy, who looks up at him and says, "Don't hurt me."

Eli takes the boy in his arms, this skinny dirty boy covered with rags, who has no food, no house, no family, and lets him cry.

The boy's arms go around Eli, then he starts sobbing. "The soldiers came," he says.

Eli nods. He thinks of the mobs in Alexandria. The picture of the mother and her son in Nazi Germany.

Even the guards in the tunnels below San Francisco and around his father's lab, in the Valley of the Moon.

The soldiers always come.

And he wonders, now that he's turned thirteen, if this is what it means to grow up—that you have to help soak up the tears for all the kids younger than you and tell them that everything will be okay.

The boy keeps crying, and Eli suddenly realizes he feels responsible for him. But what can he do? He doesn't know anything about ancient Jerusalem, about where to go, especially where to go after the city's been destroyed in a war.

He'll just have to take the boy back to see the healer woman, Huldah—even though she told him he'd have to leave for a while, while she found out if there was still a chance to save his friend Thea.

Or whether her slow pox was getting worse.

Chapter One

Eli: House of David

Ow! Even moving my eyes hurts.

I'm trying to follow the Comnet image as it goes across the room—a guy in a baggy baseball uniform and long hair and beard, running around the bases after hitting a home run—but even the slight turn of my eye muscles moves my head a little, which pulls against all the restraints and straps and rods holding me in. Holding me still.

When they told me "not to move a muscle," I guess they meant it.

The DARPA people—the Defense Advanced Research Projects Agency—are trying to get another particle scan of my body, a kind of road map of all my atoms. They say the scan will be like a circuit board, showing the microscopic currents flowing through me, from atom to atom. Maybe even particle to particle.

"It's the best we can do, since we don't really want to break your body apart to look at your atoms. After all, we don't want to turn you into some kind of nuclear bomb!" That's what passes for a joke here at DARPA, and it was told to me by a woman whose code name is Thirty.

It was the only name she'd give me. She took it from a baseball player's uniform, from a picture on a hologram card I was holding, back when I was a younger kid. Back when the whole Danger Boy thing began. I don't actually know her real code name. Or her real *real* name.

She's named after a number on a shirt.

Number 33, Green Bassett, had a mysterious past that made him one of the bearded squad's early stars. He was rumored to be a World War I deserter, but nobody was sure from which side. For the 3.3 years he was touring with the team, he always hit thirty-three home runs per season and batted .333. He said this was deliberate, that he was trying to "use numbers to bring a message to the fans, to let them know it's later than they think." Although he never fully explained what he meant, he was undoubtedly referring to the fact that the House of David squad, like the community they represented, believed that the end times were near, that God would come down to Earth, and that life as it was presently known would have a fiery end—and rebirth.

Bassett later disappeared from the squad during a trip to Oklahoma—as mysteriously as he had arrived.

So to pass the time, I'm watching a Comnet documentary on the old House of David barnstorming baseball team.

I found out about them when I was trying to find a Barnstormers game on the Comnet screen in my room, here in the old BART tunnels under San Francisco, where DARPA still keeps a secret compound. When I used the Comnet, I mostly got ACCESS DENIED messages when I tried to read the news or see if there was any mail for me.

But there were a few Comsites I was allowed to see. One search for *Barnstormers* brought me to this House of David baseball team locus, with all the guys in their baggy outfits and with long hair and beards, because in their religion, they didn't believe in cutting them.

These House of David guys were playing baseball and, at the same time, trying to end the world as they knew it.

It was one of the only times—outside of being a Yankee fan—when someone believed that the very act of playing baseball could affect the future not only of the earth but of the very heavens themselves.

The House of David traveling squad considered putting on baseball games for Americans who were interested in the still-new sport part of doing "good works"— making things right in the world they lived in now and preparing the way for the world to come.

Can the future of the earth really be changed? Can any one person really affect it? Maybe. Because I already know that if you're not careful, you can really mess up the past. Which means you're changing *somebody's* future, even if it doesn't seem like your own.

I guess the question is, can anybody—even a whole team of people who think God has a personal interest in every inning they play—really control what happens next, or are we all just along for the ride?

Green Bassett is running out from the Comnet screen into the middle of the room to catch a fly ball, and I can't turn to watch, not without

ripping all these wires off and messing everything up, forcing them to start my scan over again.

Even the stuff I'm allowed to watch in here, I
can't really watch.

*The House of David baseball team grew
out of the Israelite House of David, a religious
community established in Michigan in 1903.
The Colony hoped to gather what it considered "the ten lost tribes of Israel" in one
spot, to await the millennium, which they
also thought would bring the Messiah.
The founder of the community, Benjamin
Purnell, thought that playing baseball
would be a useful pastime while they were
waiting. A House of David team was
formed in 1913, and a few years later, they
were barnstorming across the country.*

I'm not a kid anymore. I've just turned thirteen—just had a birthday that no one noticed
except for Thea. And *she* can't figure out if she's
just turned fourteen years old or sixteen hundred

years old, depending on whether you calculate how her life feels to her or where it started—back in Egypt, in the library at Alexandria, right after the turn of the . . . what? Fifth century, I guess.

But even locked up here in the DARPA tunnels, I can still figure *some* things out.

For starters, as you grow up, you look at the world around you and think, *This is how it's always been,* and maybe even, *This is how it's* supposed *to be*—these parents, this house (if you even have a house, or if you even have both parents)—and you think everything that came before was designed, pretty much, to create the world just for you.

Even the bad stuff: the endless wars, the chunks of cities blown up with suitcase bombs, the gas riots, the last of the great forests vanishing 'cause the weather keeps changing . . .

You kind of figure that however much better it may have been before, even the bad things had to happen, because somehow, it all led up to our birth, and, well, the world was made just for us. Wasn't it?

7

I mean, that's what kids are supposed to think, to grow up happy. Aren't they? That everything was meant to happen just for them?

But I know different.

Sure, I'm "special"; I'm what DARPA calls a "chronological asset." I can move through time, become a time traveler, when I put on the San Francisco Seals cap that popped through a dimensional rift created in my parents' lab one day. My wearing that cap creates an impossible moment: The cap didn't exist when I was born, but when I put it on, the particles in my atoms suddenly race backward, which causes *me* to go backward—backward in time, traveling through the Fifth Dimension, to who knows where, or when.

Anyway, that's what a chronological asset is. I saw that phrase in the latest report in my Danger Boy file, when they were debriefing me.

I'm learning a lot of grown-up words lately: *debrief* is kind of code for "getting everyone's story straight," which is what DARPA had to do after Thea, Clyne, and I came back from our time with Lewis and Clark and Thomas Jefferson and his friend Sally Hemings. His "friend" who was also his slave.

And in an era when African Americans weren't allowed to play major-league baseball, the House of David team—made up of white, believing Christians, along with many major-leaguers who were between jobs or finishing out a career—could be found barnstorming with Negro League teams like the Pittsburgh Crawfords, Homestead Grays, and Kansas City Monarchs. The House of David was perhaps operating on a belief that "on Judgment Day, everyone will be equal." For many decades, major-league baseball made it clear that in their estimation, Judgment Day was very far away indeed.

And now there's Satchel Paige, the great Negro League pitcher, throwing to Joe DiMaggio in an exhibition game. The ball goes straight across the room, past my face, but I can't move to follow it. From the very corner of my eyes, I can just see a piece of DiMaggio striking out. He looks young. When I met him, in San Francisco during World War II, he looked older. But I guess when there's a war on, everyone looks older.

I wonder if I do. Look older, I mean. There aren't any mirrors here. Are there usually mirrors in jails?

I know this isn't called a jail, but I also know that adults change the meaning of words around any way they want to — words like *love* and, for sure, words like *time* and *history.*

Like me being a chronological asset, which is just a fancy way of saying "a time traveler who we're trying to put to good use."

That's why I'm basically in jail right now. They don't want me disappearing again.

Like Green Bassett.

Green Bassett disappeared after an experimental night game in Vinita, Oklahoma. In his last outing with the squad, he faced

Satchel Paige and, like the great Joe DiMaggio, could only manage to go 1-for-5 against the legendary pitcher.

Later, after Bassett had been missing for several days, his teammates didn't recall much that was unusual, except that when they said, "See you tomorrow," he replied, "Really? And you can still be sure when tomorrow is?"

Now Bassett and the rest of the team are kind of like ghosts—filling up the room in Comnet 3-D, projected from the locus, which tells about their history. I wonder if they knew *that* was going to happen—that they'd turn into phantoms coming out of a machine.

I don't want that to happen to my friends—to Thea or Clyne or me. I don't want us to just be ghosts in a time-travel machine. I'd like to get our lives back, to be kids again—or in Clyne's case, a dinosaur again.

Thirty, and the rest of the DARPA people, probably think they're letting me be a kid, with the baseball jersey they left in here: House of David, number 33. Green Bassett. It's a cool replica, but it's also creepy.

Creepy because it's supposed to be my reward for getting all my atoms mapped, as if I really had a choice in any of it. And creepy because it means they've been monitoring everything I've been doing in my room. Everything I watch on the Comnet. Everything I think, for all I know.

It's also kind of mysterious: There are two letters sewn inside the bottom, squiggly lines that look like this: בב.

I think they might be Hebrew letters. Why are they in a baseball jersey? Is it some kind of DARPA code? They certainly had the jersey ready to go when I walked in here.

"For helping us," Thirty said, "we'd like to give you a little gift. Something we thought you'd like."

You want to reward me? Let me know who my parents were before time travel became their main interest. But ACCESS DENIED was what I got when I tried to look up stuff about them.

Who were they before they became parents? Who else did they love, besides each other? What kind of trouble did they get into when they were teenagers? Could I find out anything that would help me rescue my mom from back in the time of Joe DiMaggio, or wherever she was?

Time travel. The thing that everybody dreams of doing: getting second chances, maybe even trying to fix up history so it's a little less scary and bloody and dark. But time travel's the thing that caused the Sands family to fall apart.

Even kids from divorced families get to live with one parent. Right now, I don't have any.

Wheenk! Wheenk! Wheenk! Wheenk!

I jerk my neck and pull off one of the wires.

They're testing the bug alarm again.

Wheenk! Wheenk!

At least, I'm pretty sure it's a test. The detectors are meant to pick up stray slow pox viruses. Usually a recorded voice comes on to let you know it was just practice.

But if this was a real emergency, where would I go? I'd have to pull off the rest of these wires and figure out a way to crawl out of this humming metal box I'm in, then figure out a way to pick the electronic locks on the door.

And even if I did all that, I'd still just find myself in a clean, bright cell in a tunnel somewhere underneath San Francisco: my "guest quarters." That's what Thirty calls them.

The Comnet ghosts from the House of David team play their hundredth baseball game all around me. They aren't worried about slow pox at all. I don't think they've even heard of it. They had other diseases to worry about.

The founder of the House of David community in Michigan, Benjamin Purnell, eventually died of tuberculosis, after an exhausting legal trial having to do with fraud and misconduct. The team had to be reorganized after the power struggle resulting from his death.

I wonder if I'm going to be "reorganized." There's kind of a power struggle here. Thirty works with a man named Mr. Howe. Or did until he accidentally went back in time with us. Now she seems to be in charge of DARPA. Or maybe in charge of something bigger that's in charge of DARPA.

It's all part of those grown-up secrets they haven't let me in on yet.

Wheenk!

They won't let me see my friends.

Wheenk!

They won't let me see my father.

Wheenk!

They won't tell me if they know anything about my mother.

Wheenk!

And I'm stuck here getting my atoms mapped.

Wheenk!

Alone in here, separate from everything, from all of history. Alone except for all the 3-D ghosts from the House of David baseball team, with their long hair and their hopes that everyone could live in heaven forever.

Like them, I'm waiting for some kind of cataclysm to shake things loose. To get me out of here.

Wheenk!

There's still no voice telling everyone that this is just practice. Just a test.

Wheenk!

And I have no way to know what to expect if this *is* a real bug alarm. If the disease has really gotten in after all. Even way down here. In jail.

With all the ghosts.

Chapter Two

Thea: Mothers
February 2020 C.E.

"Talk to us the way you talked to your mother about time travel. The way she would talk to *you.*"

"You don't look like the mothering type." I say it in Greek, just to throw the translator off. He's been expecting more Latin.

Of course, he doesn't realize I can understand everything he says, whether it's in Latin or Greek or the English he uses when he's talking to the woman next to him. They don't know about the lingo-spot I'm wearing. And I'm not planning to tell either of them.

The woman who calls herself Thirty waits for the translator to convert my Greek sentence into English. When he does, she's not happy. "Real mothers have real names," I add. "Not numbers." The translator doesn't bother with that. He just shrugs.

We've been at this for a long time. If they had sundials in this artificial light, we'd be deep into the shadow zone now. I'm starting to understand what it was like for Clyne when they had him in that zoo, that prison he was in, before I was able to rescue him in the Saurian ship.

The very ship we lost in the Fifth Dimension, which crash-landed later, somewhere else in America's history. As did we. Where we met Jefferson President and Sally Hemings, and where my friend Eli traveled with the soldiers Lewis and Clark.

And then we found our way . . . back here, to Eli's time, the year 2020 C.E. I am not sure how long we've been back. It is hard to tell time when you're a prisoner. Each day looks much like the last.

Though I am pretty sure I've had what Eli calls "a birthday" and am now fourteen summers old.

At this age, in Alexandria, they would start looking for a husband for me. Perhaps someone around the same number of years. Like Eli.

Luckily, Mother did not believe in such things.

"Why are your cheeks turning red?"

I hope this ends soon. It's getting really warm in here. And these questions are starting to make me shiver.

"We know at the time of her death, your mother was working on primitive time-travel experiments. We even know about *this*."

Thirty gestures to the translator, who carefully puts on a pair of gloves as he finishes turning Thirty's words into Latin. Then he reaches down into a little metal box he's kept on the floor, unlatches it, and pulls out a sack that looks like it's sewn from rough flax or linen.

And then he takes out the thing in the sack— and I see that somehow they have managed to steal from Mother's lab.

"An astrolabe, Thea. You recognize the design,

I assume?" Thirty looks at me, and for reasons I don't fully understand, I giggle.

And when I giggle, I am suddenly just seven or eight summers old, not fourteen, and I am watching Mother put the gears and wheels of her astrolabe together, her circular, mechanical chart of the stars. She's showing me how the circles in it turn to let you know where celestial bodies are in the sky, and when you might expect the moon to rise, in case you were interested in observing it that night or were getting ready for a festival.

"Look here, Mermaid. This shows the rotation of our own Earth through the skies, and how the heavenly bodies move in relation to us." She turns the rule on the front, and the wheels-within-wheels move. "Here are the days and nights through which we live our lives, one coming after the other—the usual way we move through time."

"I want to know if it's time for more sweet cakes, Mommy."

"Soon. But look again, Mermaid—what if we could do this?" And she takes a sharp pin and shows me a hole she's bored into the two faces of the astrolabe, and she runs the pin through, from side to side. "What if we could move *in between* the stars while they march through time? What if we could—"

"Take a shorter passage?" I finish her sentence.

"Yes, a new artery, a new boulevard, to let us come out somewhere else along time's path. Ahead of where we were expected to be. Or behind."

"In time?"

"Yes."

"Like a jinni?"

Mother laughs. "Yes, like a jinni. Let's go look for your sweet cakes now."

But now I'm in a place with no sweet cakes at all. "You took that from Mother's lab. How?"

"No. We didn't reach that far back in time. This was kept locked in our own national archives. It was built by Thomas Jefferson, based on ideas and designs from a certain Hypatia of Alexandria."

She looks at me as though she expects an answer, even though it wasn't a question.

"Who?" I ask. It feels as if there's steam swirling around my head.

"That's not funny." Thirty frowns. "Especially since he became interested in these ideas and designs after meeting a runaway slave girl named Brassy. His description of her sounds an awful lot like you."

I let the translator finish with Thirty's words, because it gives me time to consider a reply and to wipe the sweat off my forehead, since it's getting so hot in here.

I wish I could be eight again, and eating sweet cakes, and looking for jinn.

Mother used to tell me stories about jinn. Once you let one out of the bottle, you couldn't put it back in, no matter how many wishes you had left. The world you knew was changed forever, and you had to live with it.

"You will have to live with your jinn," I tell Thirty.

"What?" Thirty turns to the translator.

"Your jinn. Can I lie down now?" I touch my face. I'm really sweating.

"I don't know about jinn, or genies, Thea, and I'll thank you not to be cute with me. We have a growing situation in this country, with terrible rumors spreading from mouth to mouth—sightings of spirits and phantoms; people reported missing in one place, then showing up miles away, claiming to have been gone for years, even though it's only been days or weeks; numerous sightings of large land mammals thought to have been extinct for thousands of years; travelers showing up burnt and bleeding, insisting they've been burned by volcanoes or trapped by earthquakes in places where these things haven't happened in hundreds of years.

"Add that to all the shortages, the wars, and the bomb alerts—which *are* real—and the only thing slowing down a panic over these *new* events are the slow pox outbreaks and all the quarantines. People are scared enough about that, about this disease—but they can't run away; they can't flee. The laws force them to stay put.

"But as soon as they're allowed to go out again, the crazy rumors start back up—that reality itself can't even be trusted. And everyone gets afraid all over again. So we need to look at everything, anything, that can help us. To help *them*. And if your mother had some ideas about space and time that we should know about, to help explain what's going on, well, that might help us offer people something else besides fear and sickness. A way to make things—some things, anyway— right again. People deserve something better than monsters and phantoms. Don't you agree? Wouldn't your mother?"

It's true that Mother didn't believe in keeping secrets. "We must spread light," she would always say. "To remind people of things that, deep down, they already know."

But Thirty's questions aren't about spreading light, or keeping people safer, or making them less afraid. They're about finding things out, to make the powerful more powerful. Their consuls and officers. If they could control time-voyaging for their own ends . . . what would they do?

And if Mother were here, in this hot room, what would she . . .

Mother . . .

My mother . . . ?

Hypatia.

For a moment, it was as though I'd almost forgotten her name. Even after hearing it from Thirty a moment ago. How is that even possible?

I feel another shiver run through my body. I don't know what's happening to me. At least the lingo-spot whisperings, which began when I was at Jefferson President's, appear to have quieted down.

For now.

I reach for Mother's astrolabe. I want to touch something of hers. After her murder in Alexandria, this is as close as I'll ever come to touching her again.

I reach for it, but Thirty pulls it away. "It's very old and fragile, Thea. We wouldn't want it to be harmed in any way." Then she reaches into the same box and pulls out an old book, which she slams on the table in front of me. Pages flutter by my eyes.

It's the very book from Thomas Jefferson

President's house. The one with the picture of my mother in it.

There are notes in the margins, in Jefferson President's own hand. And next to those, a drawing he made of me. Of my face. With the names *Brassy* and *Thea?* written underneath.

What can I tell them that they'd want to hear? Yes, I have found other boulevards, other paths through time, with my friends Eli and K'lion. But so far the experience cannot be controlled. And the results of such reckless movement through the cosmos are completely unpredictable.

I say nothing and keep my eyes focused on Jefferson's book — and try not to giggle (but what am I finding so funny?). I can also see the published etching of K'lion, printed in his book, the picture, which troubled Jefferson, of K'lion running from the fires that burned my town. Fires set by people who thought they knew what was best for everyone else, too. Their laws, their rules, their gods.

"These notes on the side were written by President Jefferson himself, in a mix of languages, apparently. A little French, a little Latin, a little English. Do I need to read them to you? Or do you remember them firsthand?"

Thirty doesn't wait for an answer but instead slides the book over to the translator, who looks around, clears his throat, and starts reading out loud.

"'In all the years of combing through this book,'" the translator reads Jefferson's words, "'why have I never previously seen this section before, with the rendering of the *incognitum*?'" He clears his throat again, then continues. "'It seems as if there must be a connection to these mysterious pages, and to the slow pox outbreak in New Orleans shortly after our visitors vanished in the spring of 1805. But the connection continues to elude me. And I have never relished a conundrum that resists all solution.'

"Jefferson sure had a way with language!" the translator says, brightening. But his mood is quickly dissipated by the look Thirty gives him.

She turns her attention back to me.

"This book of Jefferson's has been stored in

top-secret archives that, until recently, were restricted even to me—'Black Box' files that I had never heard of before. And I was supposed to have heard of all of them. This apparatus, built by Jefferson during his retirement, as he apparently continued to research your mother's experiments, was stored in there, too. Evidently"— and here she takes a long thin metal strand, or "wire," I believe it's called, and runs it through the two sides of the astrolabe, like my own mother, Hypatia, did, so long ago—"the idea of time travel is a very old one, even at the government's highest, most secret levels."

I reach again for the device, and again she pulls it away.

"Or so it would seem. But I'm starting to wonder, Thea,"—and now she leans close to me, so close I can smell her breath, and she certainly hasn't been eating sweet cakes—"if perhaps these 'Black Box' files even *existed* until recently. These notes from Thomas Jefferson, and this contraption he built, appear to be over two hundred years old. Including the drawing of you, here. 'Brassy.' And yet, I'm also wondering if any of it is perhaps really no older than a week or two. If maybe it only popped into being recently because the history around it, *behind* it, had been changed. By someone. Or a few someones. Like you. And your friends.

"I really hate being left to wonder, Thea. You need to tell me who you're working with. And why you did it. Did you have orders from some other government? Some other secret department? Did somebody instruct you not to tell me anything?

"If there is a plan to invade, to overthrow, and to take over by changing history, I will have the truth. Just as your mother wanted. The truth. 'Thea.'"

I'm too tired for all these questions.

"Hypatia was my mother's name," I say to her.

"What?" she says, looking at the translator, then at me.

"The jinni won't go back in the bottle now," I

add. The room keeps growing hotter. I wish she would let me lie down. "You should always remember your mother's name."

Now Thirty is looking confused.

"Even if you won't be seeing her again."

Now Thirty is looking mad.

"We will find out who you really are, Thea. *What* you really are. Whether you're actually some ancient Egyptian girl related to Hypatia of Alexandria . . . or someone else. Why you and your . . . alien lizard friend have taken over the Danger Boy project. And what you've done to Eli — who, by the way, doesn't seem very cooperative, either. Though we're trying other methods with him."

She has a small, satisfied look on her face as she waits for the translator to speak to me in Greek.

"Let me show you something else." She holds up one of their printed news heralds, something still written on papyrus stock, or paper, called the *National Weekly Truth*: END OF THE WORLD!? it says in large letters over a large picture. It's

Clyne's time-ship, flying over the bridge here in the city of San Francisco, when we came to rescue Eli.

How did their cameras record that image? Why is that paper here, so many years later?

I'm feeling a little fuzzy, and I'm not sure how much more I can . . . retain. Mother—Hypatia—always said a fresh mind was important for a new venture. So she believed in naps.

"I think with the world end, we should nap." I say it in English. Thirty's mouth drops open. I've never spoken English to her before.

Alexandria on a warm afternoon was a good place for a nap. "I miss it."

"English!? What other secrets are you keeping from us, Thea? What else do you know? *Who* else do you know?" She taps the picture. *Tunk! Tunk! Tunk! Tunk!* "You see this bridge? There's a kind of cult that lives out there at the foot of the Golden Gate, in the ruins of Fort Point. A colony for people who have slow pox. That's the official story, anyway. It keeps most people away. Except for some preacher who's been camped out there, talking to everyone, yelling at them, preaching about the end of time itself. How there is no more before, no more after. Everything is just a great big *now,* and people should act accordingly. It's all here in the article.

"The curious thing about this preacher"— *Tunk! Tunk!* her finger taps in such a frantic way that I wonder if maybe she doesn't have as much control over herself as she wants everyone to think—"this Andrew Jackson Williams, is that I keep coming across his name in the archives, too. Just like yours."

Tunk! Tunk!

"We were able to round almost all of you up when you came back to us," she adds—*Tunk! Tunk!*—and the corners of her lips go up in a slightly frightening way. "Almost. Eli, that gray alien lizard man, and you."

"Our own Mr. Howe is the only one who managed to elude us, initially, but now"—and she flips the paper open, pointing to another fuzzy picture, with a large red circle around some of the faces—"here he is, showing up in the company of this Williams character." Then she slides the paper over to the translator. "Read it to her. Or maybe not." *Tunk!* "Maybe if we keep her in here long enough, we can jog her memory." *Tunk! Tunk! Tunk! Tunk!*

Her finger slows down, and she breathes in deeply for a moment. "I don't want to see any-body get hurt, Thea. I think your mother would agree."

What? Who's going to be hurt?

TUNK! TUNK!

The translator leaps to his feet, knocking the *Truth* paper to the floor, along with a few writing styluses and stray papyrus sheets—and sending Mother's astrolabe flying off the table.

I jump and catch it before it hits the ground.

TUNK! TUNK!

That sound isn't coming from Thirty's finger.

This *TUNK! TUNK! TUNK!* is a big clanging thumping noise that fills the air—like bells, like horns, it fills the room, fills my head, louder, much louder than the finger-tapping, piercing the steam around my head and ears, and it makes Thirty's eyes go wide. Without saying anything else, she turns and runs out. *TUNK! TUNK! TUNK!*

The translator looks at me. "What do we do now?" he asks. In Greek.

"Don't know," I tell him. In English.

Yes, Mermaid, you do.

Who said that? Mother?

I wonder if this means the lingo-spot voices are back. I don't care. I have the astrolabe that Mother designed. The only part of her that's left to me. I will hold it close while I take my nap and try to dream of Alexandria.

Chapter Three

Eli: Days of Future Passed

I've been in this room before.

It's not often I get to say that. Most people seem to spend a lot of their lives in familiar rooms. Not me, not anymore. I'm lucky if I can even stay in a century I recognize for more than a little while.

But now I'm back in room 532 of the Fairmont Hotel. Mom's old room, when she lived in San Francisco, back in World War II. But the room isn't in the Fairmont anymore. And neither am I. I'm still in the old BART tunnels the

Defense Advance Research Projects Agency is using as a kind of headquarters.

And a kind of jail.

This is supposed to be the "secure" area—that's what they said after they ended my atom mapping early and unhooked me. "We're taking you to the secure area."

"Because of the alarms?" I asked. It was one of the Twenty-Fives, one of Thirty's assistants, who was taking me. "Does this mean it's not a drill? That the slow pox has really gotten in?"

"No time for questions."

The pox appears to have spread a lot while I've been gone. After we all escaped from New Orleans in the 1800s, by time-porting through the Fifth Dimension with my Seals cap, we wound up . . . almost home.

Almost back at my dad's lab, in the Valley of the Moon, north of here. But not quite.

We "landed," or appeared, under the Golden Gate Bridge, near Fort Point. The same place I last saw my mom, who had been working on a

secret time-travel project during World War II—
or at least pretending to work on it while trying
to keep it from being turned into some kind of
weapon.

The world already has way more than enough
weapons, anyway. Letting governments invent
more—especially time-travel weapons—might
tip things over the edge, especially since we were
discovering that time travel was changing history
in ways we couldn't always see. For instance, the
first real breakthrough in time travel was supposed to come in 2019, in my parents' lab. But
after a few time trips, the flow of history had
changed enough that it was suddenly being re-
searched in secret, during the second world war,
just like the atomic bomb.

And just like the atomic bomb, its effects were
widespread and unpredictable.

I wasn't thinking of any of this when we
landed back on that tiny beach, a few . . . what?
Days ago? Or has it been weeks already?

But there we all were—cold, scared, hungry,

tired—huddled on the beach, with the wind from the Pacific howling under the bridge, and me throwing up.

Time travel seems to be agreeing with me less and less.

"Behold! The end of history begins!"

Somebody was shouting, but my head felt too heavy to turn around and see who it was. And by the time I could lift it—

"Eli," Thea said.

—we were already surrounded by men with guns. And uniforms. DARPA. Army. The same people who'd surrounded my dad's lab at the Moonglow winery, up in Sonoma.

And Mr. Howe, who helped run things for DARPA—or at least *did* until he became accidentally unstuck in time, too—was yelling at his old troops. Yelling at them and not at me. For a change.

"No! No! You don't understand! You *do not* understand!" After his experience meeting one of his own relatives in the era of Thomas Jefferson, then ping-ponging back through the Fifth Dimension, it was hard to tell if he was still "in his right mind," as the grownups like to say.

Not that his "right mind" was all that right before.

Some of the guns were aimed at him—

"Behold! Their swords are still not beaten into plowshares!"

That voice again. I *knew* it. But how could it be—?

A.J. Andrew Jackson Williams, the Army preacher from World War II and motel owner from that cross-country drive I took with my dad. And a guy who seems to be getting knocked around history almost as much as I am.

How could he be *here*? They told me he died in 1969.

Then the screaming started. Farther down the beach, there were people who were standing in the tide, their clothes soaking wet. They were pointing at us. And at Clyne, with his glistening-but-bumpy lizard skin, his torn time-suit with his tail sticking out, and his long mouth with all its very sharp teeth, all of which became visible to them when a couple of the soldiers shifted posi-tion. And when Clyne started to speak.

"Friend Eli, we seem to have time-skipped from one mammal rumble to another." There wasn't even time to agree with him before shots were fired in the air.

Ironically enough—and considering how long it's been since I've been in a classroom and had a spelling test or done any kind of English or vo-cabulary studies, it's pretty good I know how to use a word like *ironically*—it was Mr. Howe who managed to escape.

He ran into the crowd that was surging toward us, stripping off his jacket and the damp, torn-up tie he had on as he tried to blend in with the people on the beach. "Let him go!" one of the soldiers' leaders yelled at the others.

They weren't quite prepared to fire into a crowd of people, but they didn't want to let their guard down with Clyne there, either. "We'll get him later!"

Thea and I were quickly surrounded, and my Seals cap—the one that lets me time-travel—

was snatched away by one of the soldiers, who handled it with gloved hands. Thea and I were stuck again. More shots were fired into the air, to keep the sopping-wet people back where they were, and then the two of us were put into one of the vans that were parked on some broken pavement just above the beach area.

I couldn't see what happened to Clyne, but he wasn't in the van with us.

How could all of those soldiers be waiting there like that? How did they know where we'd wind up? Did A.J. know? But then it seemed like they were after him, or his group, too.

The van started up, and while I wasn't exactly sure where they were taking us, I had a pretty good guess: down to the DARPA tunnels, to answer questions. I'd had a van ride like that before — after my dad and I had moved west from New Jersey to his family's abandoned winery in the Valley of the Moon, where Dad was hoping he would be left alone to do his research, to figure out a way to bring my mom back from wherever she was lost in the time stream.

It seems like such a long time ago — as though I wasn't just a year younger then, but way younger. Young enough to think everything would always work out for the best and that the good guys always win.

For that earlier drive, they had the windows completely blacked out and I couldn't see where I was going.

This time, there was a place in the back where the paint over the glass had started to peel away and you could peek out of it.

I was still shivering, and Thea found some old blankets, the kind they wrap heavy boxes in. They were smelly, but she put one around me to keep me warm. Then she looked out the peephole.

"All your citizens," she said, peering out, "where are they?"

We'd been driving awhile, and I think we were somewhere downtown — Market Street, maybe, or Geary, 'cause of the hills, heading down toward Union Square, and then down toward the Bay, in the direction of the old ferry building or the Giants' ballpark . . .

I leaned over, pulled the blanket closer, and looked, too. Thea was right, there was hardly anyone around.

"Maybe it's Christmas," I told her. "It always seems to be Christmas when I'm in San Francisco."

"The winter festival?" she asked. Then she peered back out the window. "But shouldn't there be more people out on the boulevards if there's a festival?"

"It's usually the kind of festival people celebrate in their homes." Not me, of course, not anymore. Back when I had two parents who lived with me in a single place—in a single time—I even used to have two holidays. Not only Christmas trees, but we lit candles for Hanukkah, too. Another kind of winter festival. It was something my mother's family did when she was growing up, and so did we.

There used to be a lot of lights in our house when December rolled around.

"Does that explain the absence of vehicles, too?" Thea was looking at me, her eyes widening

a little bit, her curly dark hair still wet and cling-
ing to her face.

Now that she was fourteen, she was managing to look, I don't know, not so much like a girl,
anymore, but kind of cute, even in situations
where there was really no point in looking cute.

Like in a DARPA van, where even having that
thought — about her potential cuteness — felt
completely beside the point, too. God, now that
I'd turned thirteen, was I gonna have corny ideas
in my head like that all the time?

Then I thought about that quick kiss thing we
did in New Orleans.

"Are you okay?" she asked, leaning in to look
at me.

"I'm sorry I got you into all this, Thea."

"Into what?"

"This . . ." I waved my hands around the van
and pointed to the city outside. "All of this. Taking you away from your home, from your mom,
when she needed you. From your own time."

"That was not you, friend Eli."

Friend Eli! She was sounding like Clyne, even

without Clyne being around. Maybe we were all sounding more like one another now. Maybe that's 'cause we were the only family any of us had left. Like three kids left in the house alone while our parents ran off to the corner store for a moment.

Except that the parents never came back and the house was like all of history — we never knew which room we'd be in next.

"That was not you." She reached out and touched my face with her fingers. "Tiberius would have taken my mother from me regardless. His mob would have burned Alexandria, either way. And if you hadn't come along, he would have taken me, too. You saved my life."

I didn't know what to say. I just felt kind of funny all over. We rode the rest of the way sitting next to each other — not cuddling or anything like that — just being quiet, looking out the tiny patch of window that was all we had to make sense of the world.

It didn't seem to be Christmas or even winter, as far as I could tell. It looked like summer. But of course, weather no longer worked in pre-dictable "seasons," the way it did in the old days, so you could never be sure.

People weren't off the streets because there was a holiday, it turns out. They were all indoors be-cause there'd been a quarantine. For slow pox.

I found out during one of those debriefings in the DARPA tunnels. There was no Comnet in the bare, bright room they first took me to, and I had to pay attention to Thirty.

But this particular "debrief" was better than the others, because they brought Thea with them. I think maybe they thought if they did some-thing like that, Thea and I would lighten up and start chatting away, and we could all be friends.

"You've been away for a few months and things have gotten worse here," Thirty said, try-ing out her version of "helpful." "Problems with the weather, wars still breaking out, someone somewhere always angry about something, bombing someone else. And on top of everything else, there's this plague. Thank God it's slow pox. If it spread any faster, I don't think we could manage."

"Managing" consisted of keeping people inside, mostly. So I guess, in that sense, being stuck in the DARPA tunnels made Thea and me a lot like "normal" teenage kids in the year 2020, who weren't getting out much. Thirty said something about the government letting people out to shop once in a while, but mostly keeping them apart so they wouldn't keep infecting each other.

Even though I knew slow pox was bad, I didn't think it was that easy to catch. Maybe I was wrong.

"So what do you want from Eli and me?" Thea asked her. A translator repeated the question to Thirty—who was not expecting either of us to start asking *her* questions at all.

"Well, that's it, isn't it, my little time travelers? What do we do with you when all of history seems to be unraveling at once?"

"Why do you have to do anything at all?" I asked back. "Why not just let us go home?"

"And where *is* 'home' for the little time travelers?" she wondered with a tight, hard smile. Now it was Thea's turn to ask something.

"And what of our friend K'lion? Will you be bringing him in here soon too?"

I always kind of liked the way she pronounced Clyne's name.

"Ah, Mr. Klein. Yes. You have to understand, not everyone is as . . . *used* to his presence as the two of you appear to be."

"What does that mean?" I asked.

She never answered. She didn't seem to like how this was going, and said, "We'll show you to your rooms now." That was the last time I saw Thea.

After that, Thirty started taking me to the cafeteria with her, or at least she'd meet me there, in another attempt to be "friendly," or maybe in a pitiful attempt to make up for Thea's absence.

One time the two Twenty-Fives came to bring me to the cafeteria and I overheard them talking about Mr. Howe. They said he'd gone "off the reservation," and at first I wondered if they were talking about the Mandan village I'd been to with the Corps of Discovery. But then when they said, "He's out there saying crazy things," I figured it meant he was doing some stuff they didn't officially approve of.

That's when they realized I was listening and they shut up and went back to sipping their vending-machine coffee, waiting for Thirty to show up for one of her question-and-hardly-any-answer sessions with me.

That's what "going out to eat" was in the DARPA tunnels — me picking food from the same vending machines Thirty and the Twenty-Fives used. I'd sip a hot chocolate while she talked. But sometimes I'd ask her questions first, the way Thea did. Like, when am I gonna get to see my dad? I can't believe he wouldn't have tried to get in touch with me by now. Somehow.

It's been so long since I've seen him. I've seen King Arthur, and Lewis and Clark, and Thomas

Jefferson, and all kinds of people since I last spoke to my dad. But I know he's around somewhere. He can't have disappeared, too.

I can't possibly be an orphan. Time travel couldn't be that unfair. At least not to a thirteen-year-old.

Could it?

But whenever I asked about Dad, Thirty would always change the subject. So I don't even know if he's okay or not, and of course she doesn't tell me anything about my mother, and yet I'm supposed to answer all her questions about history and what it feels like to go through time, and then she slips in something like, "Did you ever want to just destroy the whole world because you were so mad at your parents?" questions that always seem weird to me, though I've come to the conclusion it's kind of a psychology thing, because she thinks I'm keeping big secrets from her. Like some plan Thea and Clyne and I have to change history and rule the world.

That's what's weird about life. Half the time,

you have no clue what's really going on with people, grownups especially — what they're really thinking or feeling or doing when you're not around. The other half, things are exactly like they appear and yet no one believes that, either. Everyone looks for a catch, and no one can believe they might really be happy, even for a while, or really be sad. Everybody is always trying to explain things, but sometimes a sunny afternoon is just a sunny afternoon.

At least according to my memory of sunny afternoons, since I'm sure not seeing any of them down here.

I've had both things in my life — the unexplained secrets, and trying to hold on to what's right in front of you. There was this seemingly normal family once — mine — but there were also the time-travel experiments my parents were doing for DARPA, and they all went wrong and changed history. My family's history. Me.

Changed my life from the way it was going to be. From that everything-turns-out-all-right life I thought I had when I was a little kid. To a life that includes a dinosaur for a friend, and a girl-friend who's over a thousand years old.

Wait. Did I just use the word *girlfriend*?

". . . your atomic map."

"What?" Sometimes I don't really pay much attention to Thirty at all. I eat my sandwich and drink my hot chocolate and wait to go back to my room, where I have an old-fashioned Barn-stormers game going with some paper and pencils, kind of like how they had to do it with boards and dice before there was electricity or whatever.

"A map of your atomic structure. Some physi-cal tests. We appreciate how cooperative you've been so far"—was she making a joke?—"but we also want to know how it is you're able to *do* all this time-traveling without many physical conse-quences."

"I get sick. I throw up."

"That's nothing compared to other people who have tried on your hat."

I remembered what happened the last time DARPA let some of its—workers? troops?—try on the cap. The ones that came out of it alive generally went crazy. Like Mr. Howe seems to be.

"You're not still trying to make other people wear it?" I asked, letting the question hang there and letting my chocolate get cold. Like I said, wearing the hat creates some kind of impossible moment, opening up a type of rift in your own body. But not everyone's body can take it—I don't know if mine can because my atomic structure really is different from everyone else's or because maybe my brain is. Maybe some of the DARPA workers have gone crazy because they think the whole idea of time travel is crazy to begin with.

Thirty tried smiling at me again. "Like I said, we want to find out more about your molecular structure, your atoms, the electric charges in your body . . . to find out what makes you so . . . *unique.*"

That was when she gave me a House of David replica jersey. With the name Bassett stitched in back, right over the "33."

"We just want you to be comfortable here."

I never did put on that jersey.

At least not until a few minutes ago, when the alarm went off. And the Twenty-Fives came in and finished unstrapping me from the machine, though I don't think they were happy that I'd already yanked out a lot of the wires myself.

I only had my underpants on in the mapping machine, so one of the Twenty-Fives grabbed the House of David shirt and threw it at me and told me to get dressed.

"Why?" I managed to ask.

"We're taking you to a more secure room."

"Why?"

That's when they threw my pants at me.

And then they brought me here. To my mom's old hotel room. Except this time I didn't have to time-travel to get here. This time they brought the room to me.

Or brought it to the DARPA tunnels, anyway, piece by piece, preserved like some kind of museum display so they could study every bit of it and try to figure out what was going wrong with all their plans. Apparently the room had been boarded up for years, following some "incidents" back in the 1940s.

After the time travel began, DARPA started to guess what some of those "incidents" might be, so while pretending to renovate part of the hotel, they dismantled the entire room and brought it here, trying to find clues.

At least that's what I guessed after I asked one of the Twenty-Fives what my mom's hotel room was doing here in the first place.

"It was scaring people, so we had to move it. Hotel guests started seeing things: ghosts, newspapers left in the hall that predicted the future. We don't want people to be scared!"

Except when he said it, he was looking up toward where the alarm noise was coming from and he looked pretty frightened himself.

I bet they were really afraid the room had become one of those nexuses Clyne talked about—a place turned into a kind of time portal as a result of my mom's work. I bet they're wrong, but they aren't taking any chances anymore.

"Just stay in here and don't move!" Now both Twenty-Fives looked really scared.

"What is it? What's going on?"

"This room should be safe enough. Don't touch anything. We'll be back."

That was a couple hours ago.

I still half expect my mom to show up and take me downstairs through the hotel lobby, past the actors doing that radio show—the one about families. *One Man's Family.* Maybe it's not just my family that's in trouble now, though. Maybe it's everybody's.

Everything here is exactly like I remember it. Even the pictures are here. The ones Mom drew, where she imagined how I would look as I grew up.

She had to imagine it, she told me, because she wasn't going to be there to see it herself.

Here's one of me as a teenager. I still don't look like that yet.

But I look older than in the first drawing she did. I'm not that little a kid anymore.

I feel my face. It's damp under my eyes.

She's already missed part of my growing. Already missed something she'll never get back. I'll never get back.

Thunk!

Sskkaa sskkaa sskkaa . . .

Now what? A scratching noise, a loud mouse maybe. But I can't believe, with all their security precautions, that even a mouse could get in here if it wasn't allowed.

Maybe the mouse is a spy. Or maybe the mouse used to be some other kid that wasn't cooperating, and they'd decided not just to study his molecules and atoms, but to "rearrange" them.

Well, either way, I could certainly use the company.

Sskkaa sskkaa sskkaa . . .

The noise is coming from the bathroom.

Sskaaa sskkaaa sskkaa!

I open the door.

"Aaaahhhhh!"

I yell. My visitor yells. We surprise each other. It's not a mouse.

"Friend Eli!"

It's Clyne.

Clyne!

"Clyne! What—? How did you get in the bathroom? It doesn't matter—you're way better than a mouse!"

He's scrunched up under the sink, like a kid playing hide-and-seek. His eyes widen when he sees me and he smiles, with all those dinosaur teeth.

"A good time to meet, friend Eli!"

Now he's starting to sound like Thea.

"A good time to meet!" I tell him in return. And with that, he rolls out from under the cabinet, and I can see he's in some kind of handcuffs.

"You will pardon me if I do not wave, in the custom of your species."

"Clyne, how did you get here? What have they done to—?"

Wheenk! Wheenk! Wheenk!

The alarms are still ringing in the distance, but now it sounds like more of them are going off.

"I mean, Clyne, it's great to see you. I've just been so alone here."

"The waters of happiness are under your eyes, friend Eli, and I am thus *snkkkt!* honored!"

"But . . . what's happening?"

"I was hoping you could illuminate for me."

"How did you get in here? Especially dressed like that?"

"A long tale, or a short one, depending how much empirical evidence you require." He holds up the shackles around his arms. "Perhaps we can unfetter me, and I can tell you more. And then"—Clyne brightens up, as if all the world's problems were only small ones—"we can go find Thea and all become outlaws together!"

Chapter Four

Clyne: A Gerk-drive in Winter

Now that I had allowed myself to be taken captive, was I still considered an outlaw? And was it perhaps true that when time travel is outlawed, only outlaws would time-travel?

I pondered these questions whenever my interrogators asked me what I did to "hijack history," or what I'd done "to the children," by which I infer they mean my good friends Eli and Thea.

"What precisely are you using time travel *for*?" they asked me again and again.

"Homework, originally."

They didn't like that answer, glare-stamping me with their eyes and immediately conferring with one another.

"But by now," I continued, "I expect I have registered several incompletes on my transcripts."

I was hoping this information might help them realize I have suffered, too, from my unexpected lateral detour to Earth Orange, but I was only met with more glare-stamps.

"We will find out who you really are, Mr. Klein." It was the one called Thirty speaking to me. I had greeted her with "A good time to meet!" since I had last seen her when Thea rescued me from the holding zoo, where Thirty initially asked me similar questions, only to be similarly disappointed with my answers.

But perhaps she didn't want to be reminded of that particular parting of company.

As I had then, I was trying to fully grasp the apprehension these mammals have toward Saurians. Perhaps it has to do with the buried collective fears stemming from the dragons of King

Arthur and Merlin's era, who were driven to extinction.

It may have to do with the fact that still being such a young species, the *Homo sapiens* mammals of Eli's earth struggle with the idea that Saurians existed for millions of years before they did, keeping the planet, I might add, in basic equilibrium while they did so. Except for events like the Great Sky Hammer, a nearly mythical meteor event on Saurius Prime that apparently actually occurred here on Earth Orange and drove most of those early Saurians — except for the few dragon forebears that were to survive — into extinction, as well.

I tried to explain some of this to my captors, along with the idea of this entire planet — indeed, perhaps its entire history — being a prime nexus, a critical node in the history of this whole galaxy and, perhaps, of the whole universe that exists on this plane. There is, I am coming to believe, something for both Saurian and mammal alike to learn here.

"By 'prime nexus,' do you mean something

like a beachhead, for your planet's invasion of our earth?" Thirty asked me.

"Saurians do not think of beaches as having body parts," I told her.

"We could use far less pleasant methods on you if you won't cooperate," she said, apparently unsure whether to break into a grimace or attempt another smile. Instead, she asked a different question. "When you say 'prime nexus,' you mean a place on your cosmological map that you consider to be of critical importance? Worthy of conquest?"

"No. This is not like one of your endless mammal wars over resources."

I tried to explain to them that a prime nexus was the point in a timeline where maximum possibilities and outcomes lurked. Using the spot where the unknown slave Brassy had been buried in New Orleans as an example, I told them that we had been drawn there to the era of Clark and Lewis and North Wind Comes because had Brassy lived, all history that came after her would have somehow been altered.

"For the better?" Thirty asked me.

"Well, are you Earth mammals fond of the way history has turned out since?" I asked.

I thought that illumination on the prime-nexus question would be helpful and might perhaps slake their endless thirst for "information," most of which, I must confess, they appear to have a hard time understanding even when they get it.

Usually, they would grow frustrated and send me back to one of their holding rooms, each with various guardians who came and went on their shifts, each assigned to watch me, to make sure I didn't escape again.

Such an escape would certainly be the outlaw thing to do, of course. But I wouldn't have Thea's help. She'd been taken captive, too.

We were all taken captive when we time-ported back to Eli's present, landing under the very bridge where Thea and I once tried to rescue our friend: "The Golden Gate."

And it's orange!

And while the locals probably imagine "Golden Gate" refers to the inlet from the ocean to their bay, I wonder if it's not a signal—for those who know such signs—that the "gate" may be a place where such a nexus occurs.

There must be some reason we keep being drawn back to it. And from my brief studies of Earth history, it would seem that certain structures—the pyramids, and a place called Stonehenge, near where King Arthur and Merlin lived, to use but two examples—were built with the idea of some kind of nexus in mind, a place to channel and control the convergence of past and future and the fissures between dimensions.

I couldn't tell, after we'd arrived, whether the soaking, chanting humans on the shore near us considered themselves in the presence of such a nexus and were celebrating—mammal dancing, at last. They were certainly performing some kind of ritual, one that reminded me of the fervor that comes in a Cacklaw Culmination—the end ceremonies after one of the game's long rounds concludes—where Saurians, usually circumspect in their spiritual leanings, all pray to the Great Makers for bounty, blessing, and, of course, better score tabulations to come.

When these human celebrants saw us appear, or more specifically, when they saw me, a great cry and moan went up.

"There it is!" yelled a man with rumpled clothing and bushy eye hair. "Proof that heaven is torn apart and time is running in all directions at once! And it is now in our own hands to send time and history in a new direction!"

There were more screams, and people started running—away from me, toward me. Some of them had signs, which they dropped in the sand:

NOT END TIME—OUR TIME!

And:

STOP STEALING OUR TOMORROWS!

More evidence that these sand celebrants must have been thinking about nexuses and the general elasticity of time.

And, perhaps, so was Mr. Howe, who surprised us all by shouting, "*Yes!*" and running toward the yelling man, whose eyes glittered with an almost Saurian-like focus under his bushy brows.

One of us might have retrieved Mr. Howe, except that armed military personnel were already there, as if prepared for our very return.

Their weapons were leveled at us.

"Perhaps one of the not-so-good times to meet," I ventured, looking at the guns.

"You. Don't. Move," one of the squadron members said to me as he and his two companions waved their weapons for extra emphasis.

He seemed extremely nervous. I could have *skttle-tngd* right out of there, but as I watched Eli and Thea being snatched and taken immediately into rough custody, it occurred to me that my *skttle-tnging* back to outlaw mode—in spite of the plethora of food scraps, high-end garbage, and old copies of the *National Weekly Truth* that could sustain me— might make it harder on my friends. The consortium of police and military agencies that always seems to pursue time voyagers on this planet might be further panicked by my absence and take out their fears on my friends. I didn't want them to come to any additional harm on my account.

So I decided, for the moment, to allow my capture, and hoped we would all be taken to the same facility. From there, we could decide where the three of us could go next.

Or perhaps *when* the three of us could go next.

"Later, a better now!" I yelled to my friends, using a Saurian phrase I hadn't thought of in many time cycles. But I am dubious they heard me before their vehicle door slammed shut.

I have since remained in captivity here at the DARPA facility, without seeing my companions or knowing how they are faring. Left to myself, however, some insights have come to me. Perhaps not as grand as those that occurred to the Saurian philosopher Melonokus, briefly arrested in the early reign of King Temm, who then wrote "Meat and Silence—Jail Notes of a Bad Lizard." It was a treatise that would eventually change how everyone felt about our own Bloody Tendon Wars, then raging between carnivores and herbivores. But still, insights nonetheless. The fear of

Saurians, so prevalent in mammals here on Earth Orange, at least the walking-talking ones like Eli's and Thea's species, is a common staple of their popular entertainments.

Fear seems to get them *zbblly* inside, all wound up, perhaps even *shunt-crkked,* but in a way they enjoy, which, oddly, makes them feel better, too.

I was able to watch such entertainments through the spaces in the containment bars that held me, while the guardians, on their shifts, would sit outside my cage and often watch these "shows" on their Comnet screens. There were various pantomimes and entertainments, everything from attempts at humor to startling displays of mating behavior, to long visual stories, which, I gather, used to be called "films" or "movies."

One such guard always watched films about Saurians: *Valley of the Gwangi, One Million Years B.C., Jurassic Park*—a few of them seemed to have this title—something called *Godzilla,* which featured an outlandishly large Saurian, and another, a "Comnet original," titled *Slaversaur!*

In none of these do Saurians come off as particularly insightful, well-meaning, or even approachable.

As for the slaversaur, he—or perhaps she (I couldn't tell, since the subject of egg-laying never came up)—was like a Saurian who never knew the Bloody Tendon Wars came to an end.

He ate a lot. Of mammals. Then he drooled. And slavered.

Each time a guardian watched one of these, he'd move his chair farther and farther from me, get his weapon and start cleaning it, then practice his aiming.

Sometimes in my direction.

"So who's evolving *now*, T. rex?" one guard said after his Saurian entertainments, pointing his gun at me.

"I didn't realize on your planet evolution was voluntary!" I said, hoping to strike up friendlier relations.

It didn't work.

"If everything was voluntary, you think I'd be

stuck down here guarding you? And stop talking to me. It's not right."

"Did I say something wrong?"

"I said stop it!"

He waved his gun and seemed to be getting a bit *gerk-skizzy* — that shaky condition that derives from Saurian slang for a *gerk*-drive gone bad.

So I stopped talking to him.

It was on that particular night, after numerous repeat viewings of *Slaversaur!* that the building's emergency alarm system went off — a loud, persistent *Whit! Whit! Whit!* as if an unoiled flywheel was grinding its gears and couldn't be stopped.

"I *knew* it!" the guard screamed. "Alarm bells! It's a dinosaur attack!" And then he fled, after one last glance to make sure the bars would still hold me, leaving me alone with just a flickering Comnet screen on the other side of the bars.

If he's hearing bells and I am hearing a *whit*-like noise, perhaps the sound waves of the alarm are perceived differently by each listener. Indeed, perhaps they are using neurotransmitters to feed directly into the brain, bypassing sound waves entirely. Could this be another experiment? A security precaution? Meanwhile, on the screen, there was at last something new:

SLAVERSAUR II: THE FEASTING.

But I never got to find out if the slaversaur redeemed his own outlaw status, left unresolved after his first adventure. For after only a few moments into the electric pantomime, the scene where two fledgling humans tell their nest-sire, "Pa, there's something terrible growling in the shed," my chilly acquaintance Thirty arrived, a contingent of guardians at her side.

As usual, she made little small talk.

"There's been a security breach. We're moving you."

And then they proceeded in the ritual of turning off the energy field surrounding my cell, opening the bars while leveling their beam-powered weapons at me, then clamping my arms and legs in restraints before leading me down the hallway.

"Something's gotten in, and we don't know what it is. Perhaps one of your fellow gray aliens, Mr. Klein, checking to see if you've turned our compound into one of your prime nexuses."

"Friend Thirty, you cannot *make* a prime nexus. You can only strive to *understand* them. As I, like the slaversaur, seek to understand and come in from the shed."

"I am not laughing, Mr. Klein. There is more at stake than you realize."

Not laughing? Well, no. But then, this was not a laugh-round of school students seeking to make fun of teachers during class break, either. What odd responses these humans have!

Eventually, after a long walk down several descending tunnels, into areas that grew increasingly dark and increasingly damp, my security escorts deposited me in what was not so much a room but a sunken arena, surrounded by metal walls and an outer perimeter of electrified wire, patrolled by security personnel with even more-convincing weapons than the ones who escorted me here.

In the middle of it all was much dirt and

foliage, and to my surprise, the remains of the Saurian time-vessel, which I'd last seen some two hundred Earth Orange years previously, out-side the settlement at New Orleans.

They had apparently taken my observations about prime nexuses pretty seriously after all; they had transported the entire area where my time-vessel had crashed, and where the anony-mous slave Brassy had died, to this facility. The very Brassy who may have changed the history of Earth, or at least that section of it that calls it-self America, had she been allowed to live.

But where had this prime nexus existed in the two hundred Earth years since we went through it? Had it lain undiscovered all this time? Or had it always been a secret possession of the govern-ing class, preserved so they could study its mys-teries, the way they attempt to study me, in all the time since?

Did these reconstituted ruins come with a trail of bones behind them, too?

It was actually a fascinating idea: If a prime nexus is a combination of time-and-place that acts like a beacon, attracting time voyagers — the way Alexandria attracted me and Eli — what happens if you move the beacon?

It wasn't only the crystals of the lighthouse tower that brought us to Alexandria; it was the *ideas* that Thea's mother, Hypatia, had. Just as it was the essence of the mysterious Brassy — combined with the choices made by her contemporaneous mammals, and, admittedly, the crash-landing of my Saurian vessel — that made that particular spot a nexus of its own.

Would these remains, these plants, this soil — and Brassy's bones — still act like a nexus if they were taken from their place and time? I would have to note that question for extra credit someday.

Though what if I found points docked from my research because the stranded Saurian technology was now interfering with the normal flow of Earth Orange history?

And mammals are so hot-blooded that things flow only in the most *gerk-skizzy* way here anyway. I hope I have not made their problems worse.

"This is the most secure area of the entire complex," Thirty said to me, bringing me back from my contemplated studies. "Several levels below where you were being kept. Until we find out what's happening, you'll stay here." She looked at the guardians surrounding me. "With the restraints on."

No top-stomping for me. Shackled like this, I can barely move, like a hatchling still wet with egg shine.

And here I've remained, in all the stretched moments since—the *whit! whit! whit!* of their alarm system still sounding in the background—and I believe my earlier observation stands: these mammals are really only happy when they can go from one crisis to the next.

It seems to give them purpose. It is, I suppose, another kind of dance. But not the happiest one.

Meanwhile, I have had a chance to study what remains of the Saurian vessel.

I use the term "study" advisedly, of course. The entire planet is one vast uncontrolled experiment.

And there isn't a single decent Saurian syllabus here. But as I suspected previously, the plasme-chanical material of the ship has somehow inter-acted with its Earth Orange environment and been transformed by it.

Saurian technology is being mutated, changed, on this planet. The plasmechanical material ap-pears to have absorbed the slow pox virus, as I discovered when doing my field research in the time of Clark, Lewis, and North Wind Comes, and may be experiencing a kind of cellular muta-tion. This mutation seems to be causing a kind of nervous system to form inside the material's or-ganic components, resulting in a type of biologi-cally based electric grid, or what the humans call a "computer," one that is developing its own in-telligence.

This could be something new and never before seen. Something that could, perhaps, link pre-viously unconnected types of Saurian artifacts — like time-vessels and lingo-spots — into a neural network of their own.

And since lingo-spots are designed to tap into

the neural network of the wearer, everyone with lingo-spot material could in theory become connected to one another, via the plasmechanical material.

And then what if all of Earth Orange becomes a single unchecked living entity, if this Saurian mutation is allowed to continue here under such fervid mammalian conditions? Imagine an entire planet able to move back and forth through time, or acting as a giant lingo-spot for all its inhabitants.

Would the results be wonderful? Or terrifyingly destabilizing for the rest of the universe? Could such a hypothesis come to pass?

Kngaa, a voice whispers to me. The Saurian word for "yes."

But no one is speaking.

What is my lingo-spot translating for me now?

Perhaps my own intuition? Or are my thoughts no longer my own?

Have they already become part of something larger? Am I likewise undergoing a change here on Earth Orange? Something akin to Melonokus's jail-time observation that "great shifts can happen in small places — in the confines of an eggshell, or a room where they try to lock away new ideas."

So many hypotheses to test.

"Hey! You're not supposed to move around in there!"

"I seek only to test a hypothesis!" I say as I hop toward one of the trees fused with remnants of the time-vessel.

"I said don't move! This is a restricted perimeter."

"But you were the ones who escorted me here."

"Stay where we can see you!" He flips open his visor, so he can in fact see me better. "Those are dangerous remains!"

"A good time to meet!" I tell him; it's the guard who originally sat with me outside my cage and watched his Saurian-themed Comnet entertainments. No wonder he fidgets like a new-hatch.

I try to hop away again, but with the restraints, it's hard, and I fall toward the remains of the ship, which, over time, have fused with the trees.

"I'm authorized to stun you!" It's not much of a warning, since he fires as he says it, hitting the very limb where I was so recently jabbersticked by the warrior Crow's Eye.

I am knocked against the trees and fall down, and appear to have little options for avoiding the next shot.

"I mean it!"

I try to turn away, and in a welcome bit of *merrikus,* the beam hits the hard metal of my restraints instead of my nether epidermis, then ricochets up toward a branch.

Where it severs apart the limb.

"You're ruining the remains! The evidence! The project!" the guardian shrieks, and I wonder what sort of project the guardians and generals of Eli's planet might have in mind if they were able not only to understand the idea of a prime nexus but also to harness one for their own ends.

And what would that mean if the entire planet does become an active prime nexus? Could it be controlled? And who would do the controlling?

"Stop!" My guardian is full of fear, unable to separate me from the movie Saurians that he's watched for countless hours.

But then I ask myself a question: What would the slaversaur do?

Might he try and find a *gerk*-drive under such extremely difficult conditions? The very *gerk*-drive that allows the Saurian ship to move through dimensions and through time itself?

Perhaps I can get them to regenerate whatever remains of the *gerk*-drive, by forcing them to aim their energy weapons at the heart of the ship.

I roll away toward the time-vessel, but I don't want to get too close, as I am unwilling to be absorbed by it, the way the nearby foliage has been absorbed.

What would the slaversaur do to make the guard fire?

Bite something, I imagine. I chomp down on a tree branch embedded in the ship's material. I growl and shake my head convincingly.

The guard then obligingly fires at me. I move

just enough to allow the beam to penetrate the plasmechanical core of the ship's remains behind me.

And a small bit of dormant *gerk*-drive material is energized. Another branch cracks, and the remaining ship's material starts puls—

Before I can finish the thought, I see the long colors of the Fifth Dimension, very briefly, then find myself in a small dark space, having been transported, I hope, to another prime nexus, where things will be made clearer to me.

I seem to be surrounded by a plumbing structure, however, and the restraints are still clasped to my limbs.

But then a door swings open, and I see the face of my friend Eli.

"Clyne! What—?" He looks around, making sure we're not noticed.

"How did you get in the bathroom?"

Chapter Five

Eli: Surprise Party

It makes perfect sense to Clyne that he suddenly appeared in the transported, rebuilt bathroom of my mom's old hotel room and the first thing he does, after greeting me, is suggest we look for Thea.

"Find Thea? Clyne—they have alarms going off. Everything's locked down. How *did* you get in here? How did you get in here in . . . handcuffs? Clawcuffs. And yeah, we can't go looking for anybody until we get you . . . what did you just call it? 'Unfettered'? Which I guess means getting you out of those things."

"You are right, amigo Eli. But though I made it through Dimension Five with these *snkkk!* impediments, I will only hinder your own escape *thwkkk!* It is better if I stay here and perhaps try to find another small fold in time-space."

"*'Amigo'?*"

"It is a word I picked up watching a pantomime about Gwangis—Saurians, lost in Mexico."

"We've got to get you out of those irons, Clyne."

"No. I am afraid I am stuck and would only slow you down."

"Sit down and let's get those shackles off."

Crrrrk!

Too late. The hotel door—the jail-room door, whatever it is now—is opening. Somebody already knows Clyne's in here, and they're coming to lock us up somewhere even deeper and darker.

It's hard to get a break when you're tangled up in time.

"Son, are you in here?"

Son? But that's not my dad. Who else calls me —

"Son?"

It's A.J.

Andrew Jackson Williams. The preacher. The motel owner. The guy giving the sermon on the beach when we landed back here in 2020. He was with his — what's the word the adults like to use? — *flock.*

Or, rather, a *new* flock. But how did he *get* here? The last time I saw him, it was the 1940s, and World War II, and he was some kind of chaplain in the Army.

Somehow, he's tangled in time, too.

"We've got to hurry." Another voice — there's someone with him.

Mr. Howe!

That's one thing about growing up — you start to learn there's always a bigger surprise behind the first one.

He looks raggedy, unshaven, his eyes kind of crazy — like A.J.'s. Or like Arlington Howard's, his long-ago ancestor who worked for Thomas Jefferson.

"We've got to hurry. Come *on*!" Mr. Howe is waving us on.

"A surprising time to meet!" Clyne says.

"I don't believe we officially *have* met," A.J. tells him. Then he looks him up and down. "You're not a hell demon, are you?"

"No. An outlaw. I was merely trying to complete a science project," Clyne says. "But landed on this world *ftttt!* instead."

"Trust me, anyone who really knows what's going on these days is bound to be outside the law. At least a little. And you"—A.J. winks at me—"it's good to see you again, son."

"But how did—"

It's the same question I had for Clyne. Even though I'm a time traveler, everyone else seems to be getting around a lot more easily than me lately.

"Now!" Mr. Howe interrupts, waving us on.

"Mr. Howe." I point to the irons around Clyne's arms and legs.

"Boy, they really want the two of you to stay put." Mr. Howe bends over and looks behind Clyne's knees, like a doctor.

"I was afraid of that."

"What?" I ask.

"It's the time-release model."

"What does that mean?"

"Almost impossible to preempt before the time sequence unlocks it. Sheila didn't want him going anywhere for a while."

"Sheila?" I ask.

"You call her Thirty," Mr. Howe says. "We'll have to leave him here. We'll just have to find your other friend and get out."

"I won't leave Clyne! He just got here!" I decide it's my turn to ask Mr. Howe some questions. "And why are you helping me get out? You're one of the people always keeping me in!"

Just then there's a loud *click!*, and the shackles fall off of Clyne's body and clatter to the floor.

We all look at the cuffs and then at one another. Clyne looks at the three of us.

"Perhaps the time-fold *thkkkt!* changed the settings."

Mr. Howe shakes his head. "No wonder I always thought the two of you were dangerous. Let's go."

We leave the room—my mom's old room at the Fairmont. It's become part of the government's collection now, like my family and friends.

It's not even a place I can say goodbye to. And if growing up is learning how to say goodbye to people and places and things, how will I ever grow up if there's no one around to say goodbye to? How can I measure the growing-up part of my life if Thirty and the others have taken all the measuring sticks?

"This way. Now." Mr. Howe is waving us out the door. I can see the scaffolding holding up the walls of the hotel, all the unfinished wood, the bright lights. It's like being backstage, like the hotel room is just some kind of set.

"Wait." I stop. "You said we were going to get Thea."

There's a trench next to the platform where

the room has been reconstructed, with train tracks at the bottom. The cold strips of metal seem to add to the feeling of dampness, though you can barely see them in the dark. That doesn't slow Mr. Howe, who's climbing down toward them on a ladder. He pauses on the rungs.

"We haven't forgotten your friend, Eli. But Andrew Jackson Williams has helped me *see,*" he says. "Helped me understand how urgent the situation is."

"What situation?"

"A man in a shirt like that"—A.J. points at the House of David jersey, which I'd forgotten I was wearing—"should know that all things eventually get revealed in *time.*"

"Yes, which we don't have a lot of." Mr. Howe continues climbing down to the bottom, but he also keeps talking. "I'd always thought I was on the side of the good guys. Until I realized that maybe the good guys have lost their way. Watch your step. There still might be electricity coming through some of these old BART tracks."

"Isn't that too dangerous?" I ask.

"We are living in a time, son," A.J. says, "when everything is dangerous. But let's keep the odds in our favor by being as careful as we can."

Mr. Howe pulls out a small flashlight and appears to be looking for something along the wall, something besides the old pipes and the dripping water. "Here." It's a door. He hands the light to A.J., then pushes against a handle, which doesn't budge.

"It's supposed to open right up! These were emergency exits from the old BART tunnels, in case of quakes. We need to use it for a shortcut."

"A shortcut where? Why are you rescuing us like this?"

"We're not rescuing you, son," A.J. tells me in a friendly way. "Good as it is to see you again. We have come here to solve the *time problem.*"

Wait a minute. "Isn't that the name of something you wrote a long time ago? A book? He told me about it!" I point to Mr. Howe, who looks a little embarrassed.

"There seemed to be a lot of firsthand knowledge about the effects of time travel in there," he says to A.J. "We all wondered how you came across the information."

"I told you. I was a government employee for a very long time," A.J. says.

"We never could find your records," Mr. Howe says.

"No, I expect not." And then A.J. turns to me. "As near as I can tell about this future, nobody reads books anymore, son."

"I think Mr. Howe was all upset about it."

There's another *bang!* against the door, and Mr. Howe is rubbing his arm. "This thing won't budge."

I can see his face, lined by the shadows from his tiny light.

"Mr. Howe has had an epiphany, son. That's why he's here. He wants to make amends."

"What's an epiphany?"

"Ee-pih-phany!" Clyne says, sounding it out. "Nice mammal sounds. Reminds me of words like *mustard* and *taco*."

"An epiphany," A.J. tells me, "is when you suddenly realize many things, profound things, even, all at once."

"We can't just stay here." Mr. Howe hits the door again; it still doesn't move. "Damn. Farther down the tunnel, then. Hurry."

"Wait. If you seek to open portals," Clyne says, "perhaps I can be *snkkt* useful." Mr. Howe and A.J. look at each other in the dark.

"Hold on," I say to both of them at once. "Even if Clyne gets it open, and we find Thea, where can we go after that? There's slow pox everywhere. That's what the alarm is, right? All the *wheenk-wheenk-wheenk*. The whole place is locked down. How can we really escape?"

"You mean that *tink-tink-tink* noise?" Mr. Howe says.

"Whit-whit-whit!" Clyne chirps. "Sound waves tympanically resonating separately for everyone! Brain-wave security so sound is always unique and cannot be faked by others!"

"It's a biohazard alarm, isn't it?"

"Is that what they told you?" Mr. Howe asks.

I nod. "They moved me to a more secure area."

"Not because of slow pox," Mr. Howe says. "That's not what that alarm is for."

"Then what is it?"

Clyne, meanwhile, starts to hum. It sounds like . . . music. Sort of. *Screechy* music. I've never heard Clyne hum or whistle before, or anything.

The humming gets louder. His eyes roll back in his head. Then a large *SCREECH* rips from his throat, like the hunting cry of a fierce giant bird, and all of us—Mr. Howe, A.J., and me—involuntarily cover our heads and duck.

Clyne leaps through the air, right at the door, and I notice, for maybe the first time since I've known him, how thick and sharp the claws on his feet are.

"TKAAAAAAHHHHHHHHH!"

The door pops off its hinges like a tiddlywink flipping through the air, and Clyne lands inside the dark tunnel beyond it.

After rising back to his feet, Mr. Howe turns to me. His face is doing that sweating thing again. "No wonder he's always been so hard to catch." Then he leans in closer to me. "They didn't move you because of slow pox. They moved you because of intruders. They moved you because this base is no longer secure. Let's go."

He heads through the mangled doorway that Clyne opened for us.

"But why? What's happening?"

"*We're* the intruders," Mr. Howe says. "*We* broke in."

"But you work for them."

"Not anymore. Like I told you, I have begun to see."

"He's had that epiphany, son."

"But *what* epiphany?"

Mr. Howe turns and shines the light on his own face, so that it looks like kids sharing a flashlight telling ghost stories during a sleepover. "What if I told you there was no such thing as a slow pox epidemic?"

For a moment, there's only quiet in the tunnel. We can't even hear the distant alarms.

"No such thing?" I ask, wondering what he

means. "But ever since you started this whole Danger Boy business, you've told me—"

"We told you what you needed to hear. But it wasn't the real truth about slow pox. We've kept the truth from everyone. And A.J. helped me realize how tired I was of lying all the time for a job. A.J.—and all that accidental time travel."

"How do I know you're telling me the truth now?" Sometimes you just can't tell with grownups.

"I realized . . . when I fell back in time and saw my . . . relative, Mr. Howard, that I didn't want to wind up like that. I didn't want history to judge me that way, to be part of any lies that could keep messing things up . . . for years and years after I'm gone."

"And that, son," A.J. tells me, watching my face, "is an epiphany."

"Friends . . . new information," Clyne says slowly.

The tunnel isn't quiet anymore. Coming from

the other direction, where we've just been, we see lights—lots of them—just before we hear the shouting.

DARPA troops. Coming for us.

They've found Mr. Howe's shortcut.

"And the fact that we've been discovered," Mr. Howe adds, "just might be another."

"Did I mention," A.J. adds, "that not every epiphany is a welcome one?"

Chapter Six

Clyne: Wolves at Wolf House

February 2020 C.E.

And this was where you made the sacrifice for your friends?

"Yes." My outlaw status is undergoing another metamorphosis here on Earth Orange. Which is to say, I have once again been "on the lam," as they say in their filmed entertainments, and yet I have been taken prisoner again as well. But this time, not by DARPA or any of its minions.

I am trying to explain the circumstances of my arrival to a fellow detainee.

"We were still in the tunnels, with the *whit! whit! whit!* of the alarms still sounding. Mr. Howe—"

The official from the human government?

"Yes, originally. Though he appears to have phased in and out of what we call a 're-egging,' on my home planet, meaning a profound change, like a new or second birth, later in life. So Mr. Howe found himself agreeing with A.J.—"

The spiritualist you mentioned, whom you suspect of re-perceiving time, as you do?

"Yes! He'd had an epiphany—a moment where Earth mammals suddenly veer in a different and hopefully better—or at least less *gerk-skizzy*—direction."

Re-eggings?

"Of a type, yes. But my friend Eli—"

The human cub, the fledgling, whom you care for?

"Correct! Eli was focused on his own revelations, *shunt-crkked* at realizing there was no slow pox."

Shunt-crkked?

"It's a Saurian term for the sort of shock you experience when everything you have known or thought you knew changes all at once. Sometimes, it is applied to sudden reversals at the end of long Cacklaw matches. Meanwhile, the others were trying to quiet him, as numerous guardians were headed our way, and we wished to remain undetected for as long as possible.

"But Eli wouldn't be calmed, and he kept yelling that slow pox had 'ruined his life' and was even the excuse used to turn him into Danger Boy."

Danger Boy?

"One of the humans' many secret government projects, as it happens. Apparently, from my study of Earth Orange history, mammals are unable to govern themselves without using fear, secrecy, and deception."

Some mammals.

"I remain open to new data. A.J. is an optimistic mammal, like you are. He told Eli not to use the word *ruined* when he thought of his life, because in becoming Danger Boy, he'd taken amazing voyages through the universe that other humans could only imagine. He wanted my friend to consider there might be unseen cosmic reasons for his abilities."

What the humans call "religion"?

"Yes. As our own Melonokus says, 'The universe is always trying to heal itself,' something that remains an enigmatic comment for our scientists. Does the universe, as a whole, know itself to be alive?

"Meanwhile, I chirped in that I thought slow pox did, in fact, exist, saying I had found it was infecting plasmechanical material from my home planet of Saurius Prime. It was causing Saurian material to grow extra nervous-system connections, changing the Saurian material into something different here on Earth Orange. Something new and unpredictable. Like mammals themselves."

You mean the material from your home world—which you said was a blend between something built and something living—managed to show the human mammals that they are bound together in the way of all living things? Feeling themselves parts of a single unity? Perhaps connecting them to each other in the way of bees, with unseen signals?

"Plants, too!"

But are there creatures who do not already know this? When I ran free and took down an elk, I understood I was part of the elk's life, and he, mine.

"What kind of Earth mammal are you? I can't see you with your cage behind mine."

I am of a type that humans have hunted and feared for ages.

"Why is that?"

They imagine we possess the very traits that frighten them about themselves. You, Saurian, remain a mystery to me as well, even though I can glimpse your tail, flicking through the bars. Continue with your telling.

"So the guardians kept shining light beams on us from their end of the tunnel. And Mr. Howe wondered who had told them about his shortcut. A.J. was still talking about re-eggings."

Epiphanies.

"Yes. After epiphany, he said, transformation follows. And with transformation, with profound change, comes action. Meanwhile, as we ran into the dark, away from our pursuers, Mr. Howe panted out additional explications to my friend Eli, about the human contagion slow pox. He noted that while the disease was indeed real, the outbreaks were something controlled by human security forces."

Governments?

"Whoever wields true power among them. Apparently, their grand experiment was to make everyone *believe* there was a disease outbreak, in order to practice a kind of herding, or crowd control."

The humans' leaders deliberately controlled one of their own sicknesses? Toward what end?

"Eli queried similarly, feeling not only *shunt-crkked* but angry, too. Mr. Howe had dissembled, *shll-pkkt,* lied to him, Eli was saying, when sending him away from his nest. Mr. Howe tried to reason that Eli's family was already broken apart—his nest-ma'am, his mother, having disappeared before he ever became a time voyager. And then my friend did something very un-Eli-like: he jumped at Mr. Howe and tried to choke him.

"This had the effect of knocking the lightstick out of Mr. Howe's hand, causing it to skitter away, leaving my friends in the dark.

"'No!' I chirped loudly. I believe it was the first time I had ever reprimanded my friend, a privilege normally reserved for elders, teachers, and nest-parents back on Saurius Prime. But we were being pursued. And this was hardly the time for him to wage a private Bloody Tendon War of his own.

"Mr. Howe was insisting that everyone, including him, had been *shll-pkkt,* lied to, by somebody else, usually someone above them in the human chain of command. Lying fascinates me—it's so rare on Saurius Prime that *shll-pkkt* is considered an archaic word. Yet here it seems a common mammal propensity to make things up that aren't true, deliberately altering facts for one's own benefit or gain."

Some mammals . . .

"I repeat that I am open to all new data, once I am free to make additional studies. Though my experiences in the field indicate you may be right. But on Saurius Prime, facts are *kd-fmn*, solid as the ground. You don't change them for your own good. You can't. Despite the ultimate unknowability, the opaque *srz-bnt* of things — that single great mystery where facts and science often lead — you just cannot. Because there is a common place, a common knowledge, among us, which cannot be unilaterally altered for individual gain.

"Meanwhile, I hop-trekked down the tunnel, where Mr. Howe had dropped his portable beam after my mammal companions had raised their limbs upon hearing the words *Don't move!*

"Though our pursuers had many small lights of their own, I knew they could not see well in the dark. Not as well as a Saurian."

Or other types of animal folk.

"You make me thirst for new research. There

is still so much to learn about Earth Orange. However, in the dark, I knew I could use humans' limited seeing to a quick advantage, and turned Mr. Howe's light on myself. 'Slaversaur!' I trebled, to keep their interest high in chasing me. I turned and ran into the darkness. And ran some more. I could hear my pursuers yelling, using *frk* words — forbidden language — every time they tripped and stumbled. Which was often, due to their limited night vision.

"But I was limited, too, since I didn't know where I was. I decided to trust my sense of smell."

That's a good sense to trust.

"Yes. I went deeper into the tunnels, following the old rail line, toward the smell and sound of water.

"I eventually came to the tunnel's end: a mass of debris and rock and tangled rail. That's why these passageways had been abandoned — some earlier calamity left them unused, and thus free to be colonized by the government of Eli's time, converting them to a locus with a secret purpose.

"The guardians who pursued me were yelling at me to *'Stop! Halt!'* and to generally desist in my running. They were tired of the chase and were even firing their weapons at me. I was still able to move fast enough, despite my old jabber-stick wound, to avoid exploding into many tiny pieces. Yet why go to all that trouble to catch me, if they only wanted to blow me up?"

You look for logic where there is fear and passion.

"There may have been fear and passion, but soon enough, there was water. Much, much water. The explosive projectiles were dislodging the rock barrier behind me, which had been fashioned into a sealed wall, a barrier against the bay outside the DARPA tunnels. The excitable mammals pursuing me suddenly realized the same thing and screamed the command, *'Hold your fire!'* at one another. But it was too late.

"Soon a trickle, then a torrent, of liquid came through the tunnel, pouring over the tracks, causing sparks and confusion, but eventually allowing me to stop running and start swimming.

"I squeezed my way through a small opening into a vast body of water."

Like the fish tribes.

"Yes! Like the Saurians on their water planet."

Are you a fish?

"I don't have the *sshezz-flmm,* the breath capacity, for it. Behind me the DARPA tunnel walls continued to give way. But once again, my good intentions may have caused even more confusion for my friends, and this time of a liquid nature.

"Being separated from them by the roaring water pouring in, I made my way to the surface, gulping down much *sshezz,* much air, and finally found myself under the very bridge Thea and I had flown by before in the Saurian time-vessel. The same bridge we had returned to when we time-ported back from the days of Clark, Lewis, and North Wind Comes."

Human names I recognize. From the time of my first grandmother, Silver Throat.

"Yes! I knew Silver Throat!"

You are like the Fish Man in her stories.

"I am the same Fish Man! She was my friend! Who are you?"

The signs here call me the mind-reading wolf. In my tribe of wolves, they say this ability was passed down from Silver Throat herself—that after her encounter with the Fish Man, she grew to understand the thoughts and languages of many different creatures. But perhaps I am a novelty simply because humans are always startled whenever they are actually listened to.

And is that what you are called? The Fish Man?

"Is this the kind of prison where you are assigned new names? I haven't been in one of those yet."

They don't call it a prison. They call it a carnival. It's a traveling show, for the amusement of humans.

"Really? Amusements? Do they show what they call 'movies' here? Especially one called *Slaversaur!*? That apparently amuses humans, too, though the reasons for it elude me. If they run one about Gwangis, however, we can learn new words. Like *amigo.* And *mañana,* which refers to the movement of time. You can call me by *my* name, though." And I pronounce it for her in my native Saurian.

And you can call me by mine: Silver Eye.

"You are named in remembrance of your forebear Silver Throat."

Yes. And because I am said to see things. I see how you came to us here.

"I have been telling you the story."

I also see that you have more to tell— concerning your friends.

"Yes. It's how I came to be captive here, in this—you said, 'carnival'?"

Yes. Rocket Royd's Traveling Circus and Odd-Lots Carnival.

"Do carnivals always camp in ruins? I understand that this place was once called Wolf House. Perhaps you knew of it?"

No. Rocket Royd came here to look for something nearby.

"My friend Eli's nest-sire kept a dwelling near here, a place for research and experimentation.

And it was this destination I headed for after taking leave of the—"

"Fish!"

I turn to the new human voice. I can see him through the bars. He is a boy, younger than Eli, his eyes wider, his hair darker, more tangled. He seems a little, not *gerk-skizzy*, but *klnndd*, frightened—and somehow a little harder, too, as though he is trying to be old before he's ready.

He also has long strands of human hair coming out of his young face, trailing in front of him.

The Bearded Boy, Silver Eye tells me. *He's part of the carnival, too.*

"Fish for dinner!" He has a metal container in his hands, and he throws whole fish, entire aquatic life forms, with scales and tentacles, most of them quite dead, into the cages in front of us.

"So you're the new guy," the Bearded Boy says to me. "The Dragon Man."

The Dragon Man. Impressive.

"Rocket told me about you. Well, don't breathe fire on this stuff; you'll overcook it!" He laughs.

"That is what you human mammals refer to

as a joke, correct? And as long as I am here in jail, is it possible to get another name? Such a re-naming wouldn't be allowed on Saurius Prime, but here on Earth Orange, I should take full advantage of being an outlaw."

"Eat!" he snaps back at me. "Don't talk! We're moving out. And that's all you need to know for now."

Moving where?

"You don't talk, either!" he snaps at the wolf. "I told you it spooks me when you get into my head like that! I don't want any other voices there! And we're movin' to wherever Rocket wants to go next. He said something about home; that's all I know. Huh. Like anyone really has a home anymore." The Bearded Boy turns to huff-stomp away but then turns back to us, his eyes still scared, but needing, perhaps, to talk to someone, anyway. He stares at me a couple moments longer. "You don't look so scary in there. No sudden moves, though, or I'll get Strong Bess to come in here. Rocket might be right. Maybe he's finally caught a real moneymaker with you."

The Bearded Boy approaches again. "Or maybe you're just somebody in a suit." He takes a stick and pokes it through the bars of my cage.

"Oww!" I yell.

"Even if you are a dragon man, don't get any big ideas. You're not the star of the show yet."

Then the Bearded Boy walks away. The fish he threw at me is already starting to smell.

I'll take it, if you're not hungry. Food is hard to come by here. You should try to get some sleep before we move again. We'll be leaving in the morning.

"Does that boy think I'm a slaversaur, too? Some kind of outlaw Gwangi that wants to hurt him?"

No, Silver Eye tells me. *He's afraid Rocket won't need him in the carnival anymore. He's always scared he's going to be replaced. And he doesn't have anywhere else to go. You mentioned the place we're camped now is called Wolf House. Do you know if these great ruins were caused in some war between wolves and men?*

"I don't think so. Has there been such a war?"

They have waged war against us for thousands of their years. Are these the ruins where Rocket captured you?

"No. Close to here, though. I was revisiting the house of my deep friends, and I let my guard down."

How?

"I was standing in my friend Eli's room, and it happened when my attention was caught by this." I take the folded sheets of paper from my pocket—a once-standard medium for communication between humans but now rarely used except by publications like the *National Weekly Truth*—that I found next to Eli's old bed.

It has his name on it: ELI.

"I believe this is what humans call a 'letter.' It is from an old nest-friend of Eli's named Andy. And I need to find a way to deliver it."

Chapter Seven

Thea: Time Bandits

I know that I am sick, that I am seeing with what we called *pox eyes* back in Alexandria, when I witness Mr. Howe and Eli fall out of the sky into my room.

Or at least through the ceiling. And onto the floor.

"The shortcuts around this place," Mr. Howe says to Eli, wiping himself off, "aren't what they used to be." Both of them are wet, almost muddy.

"Being swept away by all that seawater didn't help," Eli adds.

It's already quite a vivid fever dream.

"Welcome back, Mr. Howe," says the number lady. Which number did she say she was again? "We've been working on the tunnels and pipes since you've been away, trying to make them more secure. As you would have wanted, old friend. After all, we can't have people wandering around here at will, trying to extract people better left under our protection."

For an "old friend," Mr. Howe doesn't seem very happy to see her. But she keeps talking. "Once upon a time, you would have appreciated that. Especially when we have guests like him"—she points to Eli—"who won't stay put."

"His not staying put," Mr. Howe says, "is what made him a chronological asset, remember?"

"That's not what I meant, and you know it."

"I think I twisted my ankle," Mr. Howe replies.

"It's hide-and-peek!" I say, and giggle, realizing at last what game we are playing, then wondering why everyone seems to be getting it wrong.

Besides, since it's my dream, I think we should have some fun.

Everyone looks at me with strange expressions, as if they don't understand what's really happening.

Next to the number lady are the men known as the two Twenty-Fives. They had been waiting with me for some time, since they found Eli's confinement-chamber empty, convinced that Eli, and Mr. Howe, would eventually show up here, looking for me.

Here in Alexandria. In the library. Where I, in turn, have been waiting for Mother to come back, because I believe I have a late-summer chill. That's why I'm shivering.

Perhaps we should wait till everyone's back — safe and home — and this chill goes away, before we have our party.

The entire time the number lady has been waiting with me, she didn't make any lemon juice with honey like Mother would have. She did bring in a physic or two to look at me — and pry my eyes open and feel my skin — but none appeared to have heard of Serapis, the healing god, and whether I fully believe in Serapis or not, I'm not against bolstering the celestial odds in my favor by whatever means necess —

Ulp.

Oh.

"Thea!"

I believe I have just vomited. Much the way Eli does after time-traveling. Only a little worse.

Which is funny, because Eli is here and he hasn't time-traveled at all.

It's very funny.

I start laughing.

"Thea!" It's Eli again. He's holding me up now. "Will somebody help her?"

All the grownups look at one another. Finally, one of the Twenty-Fives hands Eli some kind of rag, and he begins wiping my face.

"I'm waiting for Mother, Eli."

"Your mother isn't here, Thea."

"Perhaps she's with *your* mother, then?"

"Neither of our moms are here. We need to clean you up."

"Then maybe you can find Sally for me. Unless she's left, of course."

"You're shaking, Thea. I think you should lie down."

"Sally?" the number lady asks me. She's making notes of things in a little device in her hands.

"Sally Hemings," Eli explains. Why would he have to explain a thing like that?

"She's an Ethiopian princess," I tell the number lady.

"The slave? Thomas Jefferson's slave? Then you met her, too?" Her note-taking fingers move a little faster now.

"Can we just try to help my friend? Please?"

"What do you think we should do, young Mr. Sands?" the number lady asks. "Perhaps she'd be a little less agitated if you hadn't burst in and startled her like this."

"She's not agitated; she's sick! She has slow pox. Doesn't she?"

I laugh again, thinking of Mother helping pox victims back in Alexandria.

"The slow pox plays hide-and-peek, too!" I say, remembering what Mother found out about it—how it can hide in a body for years, then suddenly appear, like the goddess Isis after one of her magic spells.

"Does it?" the number lady asks, making another note. "These days, it doesn't 'peek' anymore unless we want it to. And we certainly didn't want it to peek at you."

"Since you've gone to all the trouble to wait for me here, Sheila," Mr. Howe says while he's still bent over, rubbing his ankle, "maybe you should take this opportunity to go ahead and tell them the truth."

"You're just upset over hurting your foot," the number lady says. "Besides, which truth would you have me tell them? You should know there are many to choose from. You helped us create a lot of them."

"I didn't create the disease!" Mr. Howe tries to put weight on his sore ankle. "Ow."

"Not originally, no," she responds.

"Maybe you should help *him*," I say to Eli, pointing at Mr. Howe.

"You have a fever, Thea," the number lady answers instead. "Perhaps your young friend is right. Maybe you should lie down."

"And miss hide-and-peek?"

And then Mr. Howe, shifting on his feet, decides to tell us a story: "All right, then, Sheila. Maybe *I'll* fill them in. The reintroduction of slow pox was a separate project. It seemed like a perfect disease: it moved slowly, wasn't usually fatal, but could be—if we needed it to be. People feared it, when they had to.

"So if something went wrong somewhere, or with something else, we'd have a cover story, a way to give people a smaller panic about something that could be controlled, instead of a larger panic about something that was far more dangerous. You can't control people if they're either too happy or too hysterical. They don't listen well, in either circumstance.

"And we needed them to listen, Eli. Things have been spinning out of control for a long time. In the years right before you were born, with each bomb explosion, each new disease outbreak, each new shock—that the oil was running out, the weather was changing, the currency wasn't stable, whatever it was—with each reversal, people grew more terrified. So terrified that soon there would've been no way left to run a country, or an economy. Who's going to go to work if they think riots could break out at any moment, their city could erupt in flames, or their children won't be safe if they go away?"

"Sometimes they're not safe if the grownups stay. Sometimes grownups harm children on purpose. I've seen it. You've even done it to me."

Eli speaks and I giggle again, even though this is serious, because even as he was speaking those words out loud, they were in my head. And I was thinking of another dream, a nightmare I had, about a soldier in a field, leveling his weapon at a mother and a child, because he had orders from some other grownup, part of the dream I had during a time of war, in a place called Peenemünde . . .

I don't think that was a dream. "What kind of story *is* this?" I ask Mr. Howe.

Everyone turns to look at me. Again.

You know, a voice tells me. A voice. The voice! The lingo-spot voice is back! I haven't heard it in . . .

Centuries! Since I was with Sally.

"What do I know?" I say out loud.

"You both know more than ninety-nine percent of the so-called grownups on this planet, because of what you've seen," the number lady says. "That's what makes you what our friend Howe calls 'assets.' That's also what makes you danger-ous. You know that certain things are possible, things that would terrify most people, who want to be left alone to live out their lives."

"Like I did?" Eli asks. This time I don't giggle.

"You have a different kind of life," the number lady tells him. "That's why we need you."

"You made it different!" Eli yells at them.

"No, Eli. *You* are different. The way your body's made. The *atoms* in it. Something in you that allows you to time-travel and come back in one piece. Your body is its own time machine. We've never seen that before."

"What is it that you *have* seen before?"

The number lady doesn't answer. Maybe she wants Eli to do the guessing game!

"I throw up all the time," he adds.

"What she's trying to tell you," Mr. Howe goes on, "is that not just anybody can be a Danger Boy, or a Danger Girl." And he looks at me and causes me to laugh again, except the laughter turns into a fit of coughing, and I can't hear anything else for a moment, and when I can hear, Eli is back to yelling again.

"You blew apart my family, and all you've done is mess up the whole entire world! And the lives of everyone in it!"

"And that's why we needed slow pox, Eli," Mr. Howe tells him. "In a strange way, when people think slow pox is the biggest problem they have, people are reassured."

"Pretend, pretend! I knew it!" I try to clap my hands, and I wind up slipping out of Eli's arms, back onto the floor.

It hurts.

This party isn't so fun anymore.

"Mother is here now?" I ask.

"No." The number lady looks somewhere else when she speaks.

"When did her English get this good?" Mr. Howe wonders.

You know.

"She learns fast," Eli says. He's pulling me up from the floor, but I am perspiring a lot and I keep slipping out of his hands.

We are all trying to keep from slipping from one another's hands.

"It's all slipping out of our hands," Mr. Howe says to the number lady.

"Hah!" I say. It's a party once more.

You know, the voice repeats to me.

"Can someone please help me get her onto the bed?" Eli really wants me to take another nap, but then I'd miss everything.

"Why is she laughing so much?" Mr. Howe asks, because he doesn't understand this is a festival.

"It's her fever," the number lady says.

"From slow pox," Eli insists.

"No, from Chronological Displacement Syndrome. Which you and your friends are helping us discover," the number lady says. "Another reason we can't let you go, Eli. The time-traveling we've already done—you and your friends have already done—has unleashed unpredictable results throughout history. We thought history was fixed, finished . . ."

"But it turns out to be in quantum flux," Mr. Howe finishes.

"And whom have *you* been listening to?" the number lady asks him.

"That's why I had to come back," Mr. Howe says. "To try to fix this . . . this mess we all helped make."

"You never complained before," the number lady says.

"You're saying time travel is making her sick?" Eli asks. "It's not. This isn't Chrono-whatever. It's slow pox! She has it!"

"Oh, this is silly," the number lady says. "Look, I'll show you."

Very fast, moving like one of the warriors from the eastern lands, the number lady picks up a needle and shoves it into my arm.

"Owww!"

"Hey!" Eli yells.

"Bad party!" I shout.

"Sheila!" Mr. Howe shouts back, but not at me.

"Okay," the number lady says, quite calm about jabbing me. She holds up the needle, which has drained a little of the blood from my arm.

"We know how to keep slow pox controlled, how to detect it. If she were positive, if she had it, which she doesn't, this strip would turn green. If she's negative, which she is, this strip will turn yellow."

She drops my blood on the paper — paper like a tiny scroll, though I can't recall if there were ever such small scrolls in the library at Alexandria, and whether we ever saved any.

After my blood hits the paper, it turns purple. Scarlet purple! One of my favorite colors!

"What does *that* mean?" Eli says.

"Oh hell," the number lady says.

"What does it mean!" Eli says to Mr. Howe.

"She's caught a strain of slow pox that wasn't engineered by us," Mr. Howe replies. *"Real* slow pox. *Wild* slow pox."

"But I thought you said—"

"It's exactly what I was afraid of. We wanted slow pox as a form of control. We made a strain that was even easier to use. But we've lost control of it." Mr. Howe looks at Eli, looks like he might start crying, and everything about this party seems to be falling apart all at once. So if this is all just a dream, I should plan on waking up soon.

"I'm sorry, Eli," he adds.

"I want everybody in this room to—"

But before the number lady can finish, the *WUMP! WUMP! WUMP!* comes again, only louder, much louder. Maybe the musicians from the court are here for the party, the birthday party, the week-long festival, except they're playing badly out of tune.

The door—the one on the wall—opens up,

and Eli's father runs through it, just in time for our party.

"Dad!?"

Eli's father looks at his son. "Eli! My God. I didn't realize—" He grabs Eli and squeezes him close, the way Mother would do to me. It's the number lady who pulls them apart. Eli's father looks at her. "There's been another breach."

"I know that!" She holds up the purple paper. "Look at *this*!"

"No. I mean in the time-sphere room. Somebody broke in. And went through."

"A.J.?" Mr. Howe asks, though he says it in the way people ask questions when they already know—

You know.

"Dad! What are you *doing* here?" Eli asks his father, who is also invited to my party. "Have you been here the whole time?"

"Eli, I—"

"The whole time they've kept me locked up?"

"Hide-and-peek!" I say again.

Since this is my dream, I just want everyone to laugh. At least once.

So far, no one does.

Chapter Eight

Clyne: Odd Lots

EPIDEMIC?
OR EPIC DECEPTION?
Now the Weekly Truth *wants to know!*

It was in the paper journal, one of the few remaining nonelectronic oracles the human mammals use to transmit information. The one they call the *National Weekly Truth.*

A man was standing near my cage, reading it, and I *squizz*-lensed just enough with my eyes to make out the words. He kept glancing over, giving me looks of suspicion. That same paper had been kind enough to run pictures of me the first time I became an outlaw here on Earth Orange.

Perhaps I had also become what the human mammals call a "celebrity," a class of beings well-known to their nest-mates and the community at large, to the point where other humans lose track of their own existence in order to copy behaviors of the ones being celebrated.

If I am a celebrity now, will I drive others to emulate the outlaw life? I hope not, since it always seems to involve winding up in one type of cage or another.

I have been in this particular cage since Rocket Royd captured me in Eli's home in the Valley of the Moon. This may have inadvertently transformed me into a different type of celebrity, a performer in what he calls Rocket Royd's Traveling Circus and Odd-Lots Carnival. Specifically, if my study of human language is correct, I have become a mummer or jongleur. Like the slaver-saur. Someone who puts on a show.

We have been traveling down the numbered

roads that were once used as main transportation corridors in Eli's time, though few vehicles seem to be on them now. They were once called high-ways or freeways. We left the particular road named in tribute to binary code—the 101—and are now on a somewhat dryer, hotter corridor named twice, for emphasis, Highway 99.

We're in a town called Visalia.

For days Rocket has been telling all of us here—me, Silver Eye, Strong Bess, the Weeping Bat, and the Bearded Boy—that we're in a hurry to get to his "grandfather." The word describes an honorific title for a nest-sire, one who is once or twice removed at what we would call egg intervals on Saurius Prime, but are known as generations here.

Evidently Rocket's presence in Eli's Moon-glow home was no accident. He had been sent there by this grandfather to retrieve a scientific artifact, and having found it—and, as it turned out, me, as well—was in a hurry to return it and, he hopes, win praise.

"I think Grandfather will be happy. I'll bring

you to him, as well," he said to me. "He's talked about creatures like you. He'll be surprised to really see one."

But Grandfather apparently lives some distance away, and it will take us a few days to get there. The vehicles that transport us all—trucks, as they are known—are of an older variety, which once ran on a somewhat deadly, polluting fuel known as gas. From what I've read about gas and its source element, oil, these fuels were the cause of wars, atmospheric assaults from which Earth Orange has yet to recover, and various severe economic upheavals. But Rocket and Strong Bess converted these vehicles to run on different fuels, like vegetable oil, with the flip of a switch.

When we perform, then, whatever currency is earned goes into paying for something combustible, so the Carnival can keep moving along. Since Rocket perpetually finds his "odd lots," as he calls us, running out of money, food, and fuel, we find ourselves stopping, for two or three days at a time, in villages, towns, decaying cities, and settlements along the way.

"I don't know what happened to Rocket's parents," the Bearded Boy said to Silver Eye and me one night, when he was feeding us. He had warmed up to me somewhat when I said his unique physical trait — a profusion of hair bursting out all over his body — could actually be considered "a remarkable evolutionary step on certain well-regarded planets."

"So Rocket was raised by his grandpa," the Bearded Boy went on. "I was raised by him, too. They said my parents disappeared somewhere in Oklahoma, during a cross-country trip. The police said they got lost in a snowstorm, even though it was the middle of summer. They found me at a highway rest stop, shivering on a July night."

The Bearded Boy threw some more meat in my cage. I try not to eat too much, having arranged with the Weeping Bat to share some of her fruit when no one is looking. If I ever return to Saurius Prime, a strong appetite for flesh could make me a social outcast among the herbivores.

But I was too hungry to wait for the bat. "Do you have some fruit?" I asked.

"Why would a dragon man eat fruit?" he asked.

"I am not a dragon. I am a slaversaur," I replied. We've been having some disagreement about what my celebrity-mummer-jongleur-performing name should be. Rocket keeps insisting on various versions with "Dragon," depending on what town we're in: "The Laughing Dragon," "The Startling Dragon Man," even "The Space Dragon."

These names remind me of North Wind Comes and Crow's Eye, since their names are more musical than most Earth Orange names. Thinking of them, it occurs to me that if I ever get out of this cage, I might like to retreat to whatever unbuilt and unsullied landscapes are left here, to simply watch buffalo move across snowy fields, once all this business with a *grabaaked, gerk-skizzy* time stream gets sorted out.

"But mainly," I said in reply to the fruit question, "because of the treaty we signed after the Bloody Tendon Wars."

"You mean, there's another war somewhere?

How can anyone keep track anymore? Anyway," the Bearded Boy said, leaving the piece of meat in my cage, "I guess they couldn't put me up for regular adoption, since I've had this hair problem since I was born. Rocket and his grandpa always said I should feel lucky they kept me."

What's so unusual about a human growing fur on his face? Silver Eye asked.

"He's still a hatchling," I replied.

"Who's a hatchling?" the Bearded Boy replied sharply. He looked around, then back at me. "As you can see," he said, touching his face, "I have whiskers that look like stripes, since my hair is red, blond, black, and brown. And there's more than just the face part. It grows all over my body. When I was little, the doctors told me it was some kind of genetic defect or something, and I would have to learn to live with it. But anyway, who can afford to keep seeing doctors? See you in the morning."

And then he went off to sleep in his straw bed in back of the big truck that Rocket drives.

"He's not kept in a cage, but Rocket treats him like he's an outlaw, too."

I don't believe Rocket has much experience in treating living beings with kindness.

Now that I've seen Silver Eye's face, her voice resonates with a tympanic difference—even though there is no vibrational sound displacement at all, but just thoughts coming into my head. Every uttered thought from her evokes the deep well of her vision orbs—not necessarily silver—and sadness and wisdom reverberate with her words.

"But he lets him sleep in the back of his truck."

That's because we're such a small circus.

We are four cages and two trucks, the other driven by Strong Bess, who, with her lifting of pieces of furniture and small vehicles and whatever else people will pay to have lifted, seems to have the right stamina for the job.

Rocket has said he values portability and speed, just in case.

"'Just in case' what?" I asked.

These are uncertain times, she replied.

Given that rapid change always brings uncertainty, she may have even been understating the case on behalf of her fellow mammals. I had detected this uncertainty manifesting itself shortly after I escaped the tunnels where my friends were being held.

Surfacing under the great golden bridge connecting the settlement of San Francisco to points north, I had realized I should leave its vicinity before being detected again.

But to go where?

And then it occurred to me that I should journey back toward the lab sanctuary used by Sandusky, to see if I could find Eli's sire, or anything that might help my friends escape detention or set the time stream for Earth Orange right again.

I swam to the far shore where the bridge connected to the mainland, and stuck to main thoroughfares from there, but only during nighttime, sleeping and hiding in daylight.

Things appeared to be changing rapidly in Eli's

world. The last time I moved by darkness like this — during my previous outlaw time — I noticed more activity in the streets and towns.

There was much more motorized transportation on the boulevards and causeways then. More lights turned on, more busy-ness at the markets and gathering places and entertainment arenas.

Now everything in the human settlements was quieter. And darker.

It was easier to move without being detected, because everyone seemed to live behind locked doors now.

The people appeared to be afraid already, quite separate from any possible Saurian sightings they might have.

By the time I had reached the familiar roads and trails near the Valley of the Moon, I had even started moving around in daylight.

Sloppy science, perhaps, since it is a well-known principle that the observer always effects what is observed, even more so when he is observed himself.

And I was finally observed, that morning near

the Moonglow: first by a family—not Eli's—that was motoring away from the lab. The face of a boy about Eli's age—with curlier, dark hair—was pressed to the glass. He stared at me as his vehicle receded in the distance.

But I was also observed by a soldier who was parked near the lab.

One soldier.

The level of security had certainly decreased in the time since I had last been here. How had Sandusky-sire's lab fallen into such disrepair?

I had little time for such questions, as the soldier fired his side arm into the air and commanded me to stop.

I increased speed and headed for the woods, and once again found myself waiting for nightfall.

It was dark when Rocket Royd's truck first pulled up. He showed something to the soldier—who had been falling asleep—and was waved in.

No security alarms sounded. Perhaps the perimeter field set up by Mr. Howe was no longer working. Or had been turned off. This was my chance to enter the lab as well.

I left my hiding place and followed the truck under cover of darkness.

As it rolled up to the Moonglow's front door, I discovered that the alarm was distressingly operative. Apparently whoever this was in the truck knew how to turn the security apparatus off *and* on.

The tip of my tail caught in the monitoring field initially installed by Mr. Howe and set off several loud alarms.

The soldier was no longer asleep behind me, and the new arrivals hadn't stepped out of their trucks yet. I ran into the Moonglow, unwilling to be discovered in such an ignominious way after such an arduous journey.

I had never been inside before. I had been on the roof once but never in the very nest where Eli's sire raised him, after his egg ma'am, Margarite, disappeared into the time stream itself.

But there was no time to stop, to appreciate, to smell the scents, since I was already being pursued.

Inside, I passed what must have been the preparation area for edibles and potables, and farther on, what must have been Sandusky's lab, though it appeared to have been *gra-baaked* by a series of explosions or, perhaps, uncontrolled multidimensional interactions.

My hopes of finding another time portal here were severely reduced.

Moving farther into the structure, hearing the inevitable yelling of mammals behind me, I turned to see some inviting tunnels, cavelike, but artificially made, filled with round containers, "barrels," in which I could plausibly hide.

Yes, something told me. Almost as if a creature were whispering to me from the barrels themselves.

But before I could investigate, I heard the much more concrete sound of shattering glass, not from my pursuers, not in the barrel cave — but ahead of me.

A window lay ahead, and past that, above the tunnels, a slope of grasses and plants that led toward the wooded area beyond.

I could just glimpse the curly-headed boy from the car, running into the trees.

I entered Eli's old sleep room. Near me was a rock. With a paper tied to it. A letter.

The letter said ELI on the front. Who else was trying to convey messages to my friend? And why was he similarly trying to avoid the security apparatus?

I bent down to pick it up. That turned out to be my error in judgment. I smelled the smoke first—later I would learn this came from the "cigars" that Rocket puffed on—and before I could move, a small jabberstick hit me in the leg (the same leg!) where I was wounded twice before.

This jabberstick made me realize immediately just how weary I was, and I felt myself slipping to the floor, barely getting the letter into my suit before dreams overtook me.

The last thing I saw was Rocket's shiny, baggy face peering at me, and I heard him say, "Grandfather told me I might see somebody like you."

And then, after that, I dreamed I was home on Saurius Prime.

And when I woke up, I found I had joined the Odd-Lots Carnival, where I met Silver Eye, and where I now find myself in the settlement of Visalia, with a man reading a paper and staring at me, and Rocket's mysterious grandsire still several days' journey away.

Meanwhile, the man with the *Truth* paper keeps staring at me. He's here early, just as the town's market is getting set up. Fewer people use or trust the currency anymore, and in most settlements, they trade food and goods and services directly with one another. This sometimes makes it harder to obtain fuel. But the market areas are usually the best places for shows. Unless there's a slow-pox quarantine in effect. Then we stay on the main highway until we reach the next town.

We are still some time segments away from actually performing. The man with the paper rolls it into a small cylinder.

"I think that's why they finally outlawed Barnstormers in public. Kids were making up all sorts of video projections to scare regular, decent people with." As he speaks, he starts poking me through the bars with the cylinder. "Though you seem real enough."

Another poke. "Maybe it's a mask." And he grabs my skin and gives it a hard *zrrrk,* and suddenly his eyes widen a little. "What are you really?"

"Slaversaur!" I snarl, knowing that human mammals seek a good scare in order to entertain themselves.

The man screams and gets his extremities caught in the bars while trying to pull his hand out of my cage. I can see some blood on his pink hide. "He bit me!" the man screams, throwing his paper at me through the bars. "He bit me!" The man starts running around, holding up his finger, pointing with his other hand to the trickle of blood. "The monster bit me!"

And even though it is early in the day for Visalia's market square, there are enough people around to stop and notice the hurt man, and soon there is more pointing and screaming, and someone is yelling loud worries that maybe slow pox is spread by blood drops. By the time Strong Bess and Rocket show up, it is too late: things are being thrown at me, and eventually at the Bearded Boy, and at Silver Eye in her cage. Strong Bess is hurriedly starting the trucks, and we'll be driving out of Visalia before we even get to show them we are not monsters or apparitions after all, but jongleurs, performers, with only pretend scares to offer, so that everyone might forget their real ones for a little while.

We will be hungry for a while longer now, Silver Eye tells me as we drive along the twice-named 99 into the darkness. *I've always found humans strange, but they seem so much more strange—and frightened—lately.*

And it occurs to me if I am too frightening to entertain human mammals, perhaps Rocket will have to "fire" me, as they say in the vernacular, and then I can give up performing for something more comfortable, like outlawry.

Chapter Nine

Eli: Parable of the Healer

February 2020 C.E.

"I see you're wearing the jersey I had them send to you," my dad says to me when his arms let go and we can get a good look at each other's face.

I look down at my House of David shirt, my number 33 Green Bassett replica. I forgot I even had it on. "This was from you?"

"They told me you were . . . reading up on your baseball history."

"Did you just get here?" I ask him. He's probably come to get me and Thea out of here.

"Well, Eli. No."

"What?" I look up at his face—then at Thirty's face, and even Mr. Howe's, to see if I can find more clues to what he just said. There aren't any. "What do you mean? You just found out we were in here, right?"

"Well, not 'just,' but—"

I don't know what he's trying to tell me, but we can't really finish our talk since Thirty's guards are rushing us down a hallway. The alarms are getting louder now, and people are holding their ears and shouting at one another as we move along.

We pass Mom's rebuilt hotel room.

"I've been looking for clues in there, about what happened to your mother, after the war."

"What clues?"

"I haven't found any yet. I don't think anyone knows—not even the people who are supposed to, like your friend Thirty." He huffs it out between breaths as we keep running along.

"I didn't even know this hallway existed!" Howe shouts toward Thirty. She mouths something about "surprises" and then ushers us past what look like steel vaults into a room that neither I nor Thea, nor apparently Mr. Howe, have ever been in before.

But it looks like my dad has.

It's like a replica of the lab he had in the Moonglow. Or a replica gone almost supernova. There's more of everything, especially the tubes — the long tubes for sending particles through the magnet-lined coiled loops where my parents, and later just my dad, tried to reverse the charges inside protons.

There are Comnet links and screens everywhere, and even banks of older, hardwired computers that don't have any Comnet access or ports and are therefore easier to protect from any "unauthorized intrusions."

Or from anyone getting a message out.

There's heavy electrical wire everywhere, too, to power up the particle chargers. The small time sphere being generated is pulsing and crackling. There's metal shielding around it to try to protect the people working here.

Somebody should tell them they aren't really safe. I wasn't. My mom wasn't.

Even people who aren't technically people, like Clyne. Who knows if he's safe?

What are they still doing this for?

"What is this?" I ask. Then I turn to my father and look him right in his eyes.

"Did you design this? Here? For them?"

"Eli, you don't under—"

"After all that's happened?"

"It's not what you think."

The vault doors have closed, and we can actually hear each other now, though the crackling seems louder. In fact, the sphere seems much more *alive* than the early prototypes my parents were working on. Maybe *too* alive. There's the funny smell of ozone, and the crackling is nearly as loud as the alarms in the hallway. And there are wisps of smoke in the air.

"Stay back!" one of the guards yells. "It's already been breached!"

"Breached?" Thirty yells.

"By some guy holding this." The guard hands

a small, battered book to her. She flips through the pages without really looking at anything.

"It's a Bible," she says.

"A.J.," Mr. Howe adds. "He made it."

"'He *made* it'?" Thirty repeats. "What on earth do you mean?"

"We were trying to secure the room against floodwaters," my dad explains, "when he broke in . . ."

"Breaches everywhere," she says, "holes in everything." I've never seen her look sad before, until right now. "Just from the water damage, they may close this place down. And now this."

My dad hands a torn piece of cloth to Thirty. "He ran past us, soaking wet, yelling about one last chance to get it all right, and before I could stop him, he jumped through the sphere. Right over there. I just got a little piece of his pants."

"You ran to tell *her*?" I ask again, pointing to Thirty, glaring at my dad. "You've been working here this whole time and have known I was locked up, and you go to see *her*?"

"Eli, I—" My dad looks around, a little scared,

a little confused, but I can't believe my own father would betray me, would sell me out like this. "Eli . . . they told me you had slow pox."

"They told you *what*?"

"That I couldn't see you. That you were contagious."

"And you *believed* them?"

"They had guards with me the whole time. I couldn't get any Comnet messages out. They even checked that jersey, to make sure I didn't write anything in it."

"We decided it'd be all right for him to give you a Christmas present," Thirty says glumly.

"Is it Christmas?" I ask.

"Eventually," she says. She doesn't seem happy at all.

"Eli," my dad continues, "in all this disruption, this was the first chance I had to go down the hallway *by myself*. I wasn't sure where they were keeping you. But I didn't want anything to go wrong while you were here."

"So you were a prisoner, too?"

"That's enough, Sandusky." Thirty is rubbing her forehead, like she has the world's most terrible headache. "After all, we let you see him, from time to time."

"They let me watch you," my dad says. "Through the monitors. It looked like you were getting better!" he adds, trying to brighten up the whole weird, painful situation.

"How could you still work for them, after all they've done to our family?" I ask him. "You? Of all people."

He's not trying to make the best of anything now. His eyes are wet. He reaches into his pocket and takes out a soggy, crumpled piece of paper. It's a crayon-and-marker drawing I made, back when I was little. Barnstormer Robot Man. It seems to be covered in . . . plasmechanical goo.

My dad lowers his voice. "I took this from storage. They retrieved it with the wreckage of your friend's ship. I kept it in my shirt. Here." He taps his chest. By his heart.

That's so corny.

So how come my eyes are wet, too?

"I found it when they let me use—"

"That's classified, Sands!" Thirty shouts, coming over to us. She grabs the paper out of my dad's hands. "So is that."

"I was using the alien technology," my dad says to me.

"That's enough!"

"Saurian technology?" I ask, starting to figure out why this secret base feels even more secret, even more like a prison, than it did before.

"To perfect it."

"Stop, Sands. Right now."

"Perfect what?"

"Time travel, Eli. I didn't know you were coming back! I didn't know if I would *see* you again! I came here because I thought it was my only chance to—"

Beep. Beep.

"Chance to what?"

Mr. Howe, meanwhile, has been looking through A.J.'s Bible, going carefully through the pages that were the most bent and wrinkled. Then he stops, and his face goes white.

Beep.

Thirty takes a small Comphone out of her pocket. She forgets to put it on "shield," because the face of the man she's talking to pops out and hovers in front of her.

Sszzzt.

The time sphere is still crackling, and she turns away from it.

"Yes, sir?" she asks.

There's yelling from the little holographic man, but it's the kind of yelling people do when they're scared, and I hear things like "emergency," "shut down," "direct orders," "panic," "control," and even the word *fear,* and when it's over, Thirty just looks more tired than anything else.

"That was headquarters," she says after a moment. "History, as we know it, seems to be falling apart. To a degree we may not be able to control. Apparently, something has even happened to the Bible."

She looks toward Mr. Howe, who is still holding the book and not moving, except when he manages to get the word *look* out of his mouth.

He's not even sure who to pass the book to.

I take it before Thirty can. It has old-fashioned color plates in it, the kind that don't move, to illustrate all the Bible stories. One page is titled "Jeremiah and the Rebuilder, Standing in the Ruins."

There's a picture of this Jeremiah, who I know was one of those old Bible guys, though I'm not exactly sure which one. I remember that Noah had the ark, and David had the slingshot. But which one was Jeremiah?

Next to him, in the picture, is the one called "the Rebuilder."

In the illustration, it looks like A.J. A.J. as someone imagined him dressed in old-time clothes. Real old-time clothes — like way before Thea's time.

My dad takes the book from me, and then eventually Thirty looks at it, but it's Mr. Howe who actually starts reading out loud the text that goes with the picture:

"The Rebuilder came when
everything was broken.
'I am a small man,' he said,
'but who will start setting stones
with me
one upon the other?'"

"That's not in the Bible," he says to himself. He looks up at the rest of us. "That's not supposed to be in here." He seems to be shaking a little bit.

Thirty thumbs through the book now. "Second Jeremiah?" she says. "There is no book of Second Jeremiah. Only one. And Jeremiah disappears at the end of it." She shakes her head. "Nobody will believe anything," she adds, "if this keeps up."

"Nobody will believe us anymore, anyway," Mr. Howe says, "after they find out everything we've done in secret."

"You believed us," she says to him.

"And then, Sheila, I woke up."

Beep. Beep. Beep.

The Comphone again.

"Yes, sir?"

Whoever her boss is, he's yelling at her some more. She sighs, then finally hangs up without saying goodbye.

"He just received a report from an archaeological dig in Israel. In Jerusalem. They found a piece of mirror with the word FAMILY on it. In English. That wasn't the only thing: a crumpled page of Bible text, also in English. A scrap of paper, like a piece from one of the Dead Sea Scrolls. Except this was from a book."

"Is he sure?" my dad asks. "It's probably recent. Tourists still go there, even after the war."

"It was found hundreds of feet down. Meaning the mirror and the book are each nearly three thousand years old. From a time when there was no English, when there weren't any mirrors, when they weren't printing any books. Let alone a Bible they were still busy living out."

"It could be a hoax."

"The page even has a number: 278."

Mr. Howe flips through the pages in A.J.'s Bible. "Page 278," he announces, almost like he's won a contest or something, "is missing from this book!"

Dad lets out a big sigh. "We were trying to control the time sphere, the parameters, how far back the fold in spacetime went," he says slowly. "Running simple experiments with what your friend Clyne calls a 'chrono-compass,' to see if we could control, or pinpoint—"

"I mean it, Dr. Sands."

"Mean what, Sheila?" my dad asks. "I'm talking to my son. That's the only thing that means anything right now."

Thirty doesn't say anything, but sits down instead. Except there isn't a chair, and she plops down on the floor.

"As far as we could tell," Dad tells me, "the dimensional rift we were working with stretched back about twenty-five hundred years—back to the time of the Bible."

"You mean A.J. just jumped through? And landed there?" I ask.

Thirty doesn't seem to mind being on the ground. She puts her hands on her knees and rests her chin. Like a kid. Before this moment, I could never imagine her doing anything "like a kid."

The two Twenty-Fives run over to her.

"No, no, no," she says, waving them away. "Just leave me where I am. And bring me something."

"What do you need?" one of them asks.

She nods toward me. "His hat. Bring the young man his hat. Suddenly, we have another job for him."

Chapter Ten

Eli: Gehenna-spawn

"This feels a little like Alexandria," Thea tells me.

And if she means a place with stone buildings, rock-lined streets, and no lights, she's right. I can't see where we are. But it's cold here. A lot colder than Alexandria.

Though my face suddenly feels warm . . .

Quickly, I'm on the ground, upchucking. Even the fancy cleaning and repair that the DARPA folks gave to my cap, and the new automatic Thickskin apparatus that allows me to keep wearing it on my head without direct skin-to-wool contact, can't change any of that.

Time travel still makes me nauseous.

But I don't have time to think about that. When I double over, I'm surprised that my hands land in snow. Not a lot of it, not like what you'd get at Fort Mandan or someplace. But still, it's snow.

I never heard of snow in any of these hot, dry Bible places. Maybe all this prime-nexus business didn't work out like they thought, and I'm somewhere cold, like, I don't know, ancient Norway or Sweden.

I guess we'll know if the Vikings show up.

"Is this Yerushalayim?" Thea asks. She says it differently, even through the lingo-spot.

I get back to my feet in time to steady her. "I hope so."

And now the Vikings—or somebody—are showing up. A bunch of somebodies, moving in the dark. They're groups of shadows and light, holding the only shiny things—besides the moon and the stars—glinting in the night dark right now: spear tips, catching the reflection of torches.

Torches held by people who are heading right at us.

Whoever they are, Thea's right—this part really is like Alexandria.

They're yelling at us, though they're still too far for me to understand what they're saying. Calling us names, maybe. Strange names, like "Philadelphians." What's wrong with Philadelphia? The A's came from there, and even the Phillies have had a couple of good years.

Wait, no. The word is *Philistines.*

And . . . *Hitters?* No—*Hittites.* And *Babylonians.*

Bible names. I've heard A.J. use them. Groups of people who lived a long time ago and then died out, which is exactly what I hope Thea and I are not about to do.

The spear-holders and the torch-carriers close in on us, and in the firelight, I'm seeing that maybe this isn't like Alexandria after all.

These aren't professional soldiers. These aren't Vikings, either. This doesn't even seem like the kind of mob Tiberius had following him when he came after Thea and her mother.

In fact, the spears aren't really all even spears. In the torchlight, I can see people's ragged clothes, and how their weapons look like they were put together with rocks and splintered wood and strips of leather, like something out of an old caveman cartoon or something, except those shows were funny and this isn't.

These people are scared. Not cartoon-pretend getting-up-again-after-being-knocked-down scared, but the real thing.

Whoever these people are, they're as afraid of us as we are of them.

"She's Gehenna-marked," someone whispers. They're looking at Thea.

The place where they dug up A.J.'s missing Bible page was originally for the "Gehenna-marked," according to the words scratched into nearby stones. A translation of the symptoms described the "slowly unfolding fever that consumes the afflicted in the permanent fire of their visions."

Symptoms that make it sound a lot like slow pox.

That's what Thirty told me right before I left: " 'Behold, I will bring healing and cure, and I will cure them.' "

It was one of the lines from Jeremiah, circled on A.J.'s missing three-thousand-year-old page, which was found near the scratched stones. Was he talking about slow pox?

"Get her," another voice hisses now. "No more Gehenna-spawn. No more strangers. We've suffered enough."

With their torches and their homemade spears and their underfed faces, the crowd starts to move toward us. They're still scared of us, but the fear has shifted, and now we're just something they want to stamp out, to destroy, the way grownups do when they think destroying something will make them feel better.

And behind them are even more people, faces I can't make out in the flames.

This could be bad. And frankly, things have already been hard enough.

But I guess sometimes you don't get a choice. Maybe that's what my dad was trying to tell me.

"No," a voice says. "No."

There's a figure moving on the hill behind the crowd. A shadow.

Some of the heads turn.

"Not her," the voice says again.

The fear doesn't go out of the crowd, but their words are mixed with a kind of excitement when they recognize the speaker: "It's Jeremiah! Jeremiah's here! He came back!"

Jeremiah was the one in the picture with A.J. The prophet. He steps even closer to the torchlight, and now I can see his face. He doesn't look like the painting in the Bible. In those pictures, they make it look like everyone has time to see a barber and keep their clothes washed.

Instead, Jeremiah's hair looks stringy, like he's been camping out for, I don't know, two years or so, and from what I can see of his eyes in this light, they look like someone keeps waking him out of a good night's sleep, over and over.

He's wrapped up in a really big shawl or cape or something. Robes, maybe, that have also been out camping for two years. And because it's cold, everyone has their clothes pulled around them tight.

"Take this one to the Rebuilder."

The Rebuilder! A.J.! Great. Unbelievable! We can see A.J., find out what he's been doing here, and whether he's learned anything about curing slow pox. Then we can bring him back with us. The easiest time-travel job ever.

Before we left to come here, I'd already told them I wasn't going to go to ancient Jerusalem without Thea. Because trying to help her slow pox is the only reason I still have for going anywhere.

Well, that and trying to find my mom.

Other guys who have both mom and girl-friend problems at least have everybody living in the same century.

But of course Thea's not my girlfriend. But it's kind of my fault she's unstuck in time, so I'm responsible for her. That's what I told my dad, right before I left again. I also told him he could come with us, too.

"I can't, Eli," he said to me. "My job is to try to fix things from this end." While he was speaking, Thea kept almost slipping out of my arms, like she was asleep or about to pass out. I kept pulling her closer, so I wouldn't drop her. "Why are you so red?" my dad asked. "Are you hot or something?"

"It's nothing. Look, how come whenever you or Mom have a chance to just fix our family, to reunite everybody, you always say no?"

"I need to perfect time travel *now,* Eli. So we can undo all of its effects, undo everything that's happening."

"That's what Mom said, too."

"And when we do that—me here, and she, wherever she is—when we do that, then it will be that much easier to find your mother and bring her back. And then she can stay put. And so can you."

"What you're doing," Thirty added, "is you're buying us more . . . time." She said it like she was trying, for once, to sound a little bit glad about something, but you could tell it didn't come naturally. "And if you can find a cure for this strain of slow pox—"

"Because *we* can't," Mr. Howe added in a sharp voice. "Not anymore."

"Then you're helping your friend," Thirty finished. Then she and Mr. Howe stared at each other for a moment. "And the rest of us, too."

Beep. Beep. Her Comphone kept going off, but she'd stopped answering it and kept talking to me.

"Come back to us, Eli. Help us get all this straightened out. If people lose faith that things work out, that life makes sense, or that it's even safe to *be* alive . . ." Thirty shook her head. "We thought with slow pox, that by creating a great and terrible challenge people could see us triumph over, prevail . . . that we could still control . . ." She looked at Thea, then back at Mr. Howe. "But yes, we can't even control that anymore."

"I'm not sure we ever could, Sheila," Mr. Howe added.

"But people need faith in . . . *something*," she said.

My dad's eyes were still wet, like they'd been since he first saw me. "Just so you know, if I thought they were forcing you to go, I wouldn't let it happen. But this time, I know you're choosing it."

I nodded. "They said Thea has a different kind of strain . . . that they thought was extinct. They can't cure it in a lab. This is for her. She'd do it for me."

"Is Mother back yet?" Thea asked. "She used to call me 'Mermaid.'"

I pulled her close, put on the cap, and everything winked out. She and I were pulled across the Fifth Dimension, past every color you could imagine—and some that you can't—stretching out, surrounding you, slowing you down, speeding you up . . .

. . . and then, there we were, at night, in the snow. In Jerusalem.

Dad wasn't sure we'd follow the same "trail" back through time that A.J. did, because we were using my hat instead of jumping through a floating time sphere. But I remembered what

Clyne said about certain times and places acting like beacons, because they were so disruptive. Kind of like a giant boulder or log in a stream, drawing everything toward it.

Dad said he would use the chrono-compass he was working on to keep the portal open as long as he could.

"But we're not jumping through there, Dad," I told him. "We're using my cap. I have to hold on to Thea. She's in no shape to jump anywhere. Especially a distance of two or three thousand years."

"I know. But think of it like keeping both ends of a slide open."

"I was thinking of streams."

"Or a moving stream. You don't have to step into it off the same dock." He smiled at me. "Let's sit down and talk about time travel when you get back."

"Let's sit down and just talk," I said.

"I'd like that," he answered.

So the stream, the slide, whatever you want to call it, worked, and so did the Seals cap, and we all seem to have landed in the same place. And, it seems, the same time, since they're taking us to the Rebuilder now.

I hope. I heard that name mentioned when they kept talking about "strangers."

Torches are used to guide us now instead of making us easier targets, though Thea is having a harder and harder time of it, stumbling over rocks, seeing things that aren't here. And there are a lot of rocks — boulders, rubble, ruined walls, the remains of smashed or burned buildings — to stumble over.

The bones of an entire city.

"Was there an earthquake?" I ask, hoping that was the explanation. Hoping this wasn't done on purpose, but being pretty sure it was.

Everybody looks at one another, then back at me. Right. The lingo-spot. I can understand them. But they can't understand me.

Then Thea speaks to them. In their own tongue. Hebrew. I think they all spoke Hebrew, at least until Jesus came along, and then they spoke Christian or English or whatever.

I know Thea speaks a bunch of languages—when she's well. But is she able to make any sense now, in the condition she's in? Because it sounds like she was asking about—

"We weren't aware this was your birthday celebration, young woman."

Okay, so she's not making sense. But all the people holding torches stop and look at us, and one of the men speaks to her.

"We don't expect anyone to be celebrating anything in Jerusalem again for years to come," the man says. "Maybe not even in our lifetimes. Though Jeremiah has promised that celebrations will come again. A jubilee year. Though probably not for us. For years, he warned us that our country would fall because we were ignoring the things God wanted us to do."

"And what did your god desire?"

Thea's question throws them off. The man points into the darkness, almost dropping his torch. In the light, I can't see anything but more burnt timbers and broken walls. "At one time, we thought God desired this. This was our temple.

The one God asked King Solomon to build. They say his father, King David, could have built it, but he had too much blood on his hands."

"It is hard to face your god when you are covered in someone else's blood."

The man holds the torch closer to Thea's face. "Who are you, another stranger, to say such things?"

Thea doesn't seem worried. I guess one thing about slow pox is you're not so concerned about being polite.

"I am not trying to make your wounds more grievous," she tells him. "It is just that birthday parties and whole cities turn very angry when people pit their gods against each other."

"You talk in riddles," the man says. "Perhaps you imagine you are a prophet, too? Jerusalem has no need for more of those." There's more anger in his voice. "People came here for Passover offerings in the spring, and for the New Year festival in the fall. What we wanted was God's favor, some way to make it go easier for those of us who had so little. But most of us were left to watch and to smell the meat when the rich would bring their best animals for slaughter on the altar here.

"What did our god desire?" the man repeats, getting even madder. "Jeremiah told us that it wasn't the animals' burning flesh or the flasks of fine olive oil left with the priests—it was the way we behaved toward our fellows. We had stopped considering our 'fellows' at all and grew concerned only about ourselves.

"But if we no longer cared enough about one another, how could we truly care about anything else? How could we protect our temple? So when the Babylonians came, the city was that much easier to destroy. And so was the temple." He waves the torch over the ruins, and the moving shadows over all the broken, jagged edges make it seem like there's still an army of ghosts on the loose. "They took everything out of it—all the gold and jewels they could carry. They took the treasures, and they took the rest of the people—rounded them up as slaves. Everyone and everything but us. To the Babylonian soldiers, we seemed worthless."

"Why?" Thea asks. She looks around when she talks, and I wonder if she thinks this is just one big fever dream. The man has resumed walking; I have to pull her along to keep up with him and the group of torches.

"We are the poorest of the poor," he says to her, speaking into the flickering dark. "Slaves, beggars, cripples, the very young, the very old. In their eyes, we are of no value."

"Then those soldiers need new eyes." Thea reaches out and brushes her fingers over the man's face. Sometimes it's hard to tell if the slow pox is making her say crazy things or words that actually make a lot of sense, if you could stop and think about them. But nobody seems to have that much time.

The man brushes Thea's hand away. Then he wipes his face, like maybe some snow got on it.

"Here." He steps away from Thea and points. We seem to have come to the mouth of a kind of staircase or tunnel. I hear water go past us. "The Gihon Tunnel. The Healer's down there."

"The Healer? But what about the Rebuilder?" And why does everyone here have a title?

Nobody answers, of course. My English just seems like some bizarre tongue to them.

The torch man hands me the light. "Move carefully. The rocks are wet. But the path will take you to her."

"Can't you come with us?" I really don't want to hold Thea and the torch at the same time. By myself. On wet stairs. In a destroyed city. At night.

"I do not understand your words, stranger. But all who are down there are Gehenna-marked in some way. You can choose to be with them, like she will be, if you wish."

Thea seems to feel the warm flames near her face. "Too hot," she says. "No sun."

"No sun," I repeat to her softly, moving the fire away from her.

I hold Thea with one arm and a torch with the other, and head into the dark tunnel, hoping to find a healer I don't even know, who may not be able to help me at all.

Chapter Eleven

Clyne: Reenter the Dragon

And so it went, skirmishes and confrontations, through towns and over roads and even in the large metropolis that humans have named for celestial beings called angels. I expected, in a "City of Angels," to perhaps find enlightenment or, at least, according to what I know of Earth Orange's angel stories, a more cosmological perspective on events.

We did manage to perform part of a show on a roadway named for a long vanished forest—Hollywood Boulevard—where we were not the only costumed or performing creatures plying our wares. Silver Eye read minds; Strong Bess bent various metals, tore thick books, and lifted spectators up by the palm of her hand; the Bearded Boy let other children tug on his long tendrils of body hair in exchange for small pieces of currency; and the Weeping Bat flew, just like the winged Saurians back home, using her radar — for a price — to find items that customers had recently lost, or to bring back things they secretly desired but never told anyone about.

Sometimes, depending on the object, this would cause great embarrassment among the patrons.

An older woman, a "grandmother" in earth terms, was given a toy, a "doll," that she'd apparently desired her whole life. She burst into tears, and nobody was sure where the bat had found the doll. Occasionally, the guardians and constabulary ask uneasy questions about such things.

"Why is the bat always sad, then, if she helps people recover lost items?" I asked Silver Eye one evening. "Things they desire?"

Because, if you ask her, she will tell you that much more has been lost than people know.

When the municipal armed guardians came around and started asking the performers for their identity cards and official papers, Rocket cut the show short—our first real performance in days—and had us moving along before we could finish collecting revenues.

I did not even get to do my new act, which involves the wearing of a suit called a "tuxedo," human clothes that are supposed to denote "class" or "elegance," according to Rocket. He says he's trying out a new act entitled "The Debonair Dragon," because "that might be less frightening, and people seem plenty scared already."

I am supposed to sit at a table—my leg is always discreetly in chains, though, to prevent my running away (which will not be truly possible until full recovery is made from my reinjured jabberstick wound)—wearing this "tuxedo" and conversing with anyone willing to pay to have a conversation.

Few have been willing.

"You never used to have to follow so many rules," Rocket complains as we pack up the Odd-Lots Carnival and prepare to drive away. "Like hanging out yellow flags to prove you are pox-free, and having to wait for an inspection in each new town you go to." He shakes his head. "I can't wait until we get to Grandfather's. He says he has a way to make us rich."

"'Us'?" the Bearded Boy asks hopefully.

"Me and him," Rocket corrects. "The rest of you will be on your own, Whiskers."

"I have a name."

"All right, then: Bearded Boy."

"A real name: It's James. James Rodney."

This is surprising, the Bearded Boy standing up for himself like this.

"When I found you, Whiskers, you had no name. At least, no one around to call you anything but Whiskers."

"Well, I'm James, and I'm eleven years old. I think."

"You think? Then how can you even be sure

who you are? If you really want to find out, I can always send you back to the streets."

The exchange sends the Weeping Bat into what looks like a *skyyttl* dance, searching for lost things, and for the rest of the trip, the Bearded Boy is quiet, even when bringing dinner in for Silver Eye and me.

It only takes two or three more solar cycles, as we head down a road coded with both binary and a letter: the I-10. We are going now straight to Grandfather's.

The weather grows hotter and dryer, and I am happy to get out of this "tuxedo" Rocket put me in some time ago, as we aren't doing any more shows, and return to my chrono-suit. Even though it has become a little tattered since I've been on Earth Orange, the material is much better de-signed to respond properly to the weather.

And then, after more travel down the binary highway, we are there.

What is unusual is that, out of all the humans on Earth Orange, Rocket's grandfather is some-one I already know.

His name is Rolf Royd; he used to work for a group calling itself the Third Reich. Eli's nickname for him was the Dragon Jerk kid, though I don't believe Rolf ever met a dragon firsthand. How the name for these poor Earth-bound Saurians gets dragged through the mud!

"You again," Rolf says to me, not in Eli's English but in the Reich's tongue, when the Odd-Lots Carnival pulls up at last, the trucks sputtering to a stop a few yards away from his dwelling, as they use up the last of their fuel.

His hair is still white, but thinner now, and his mammalian epidermis shows signs of having aged since we last encountered each other in the Fifth Dimension, after leaving Arthur the king and Merlin the wizard behind us.

Eli, Thea, and I wound up back in the time of Lewis and Clark, as did my time-vessel. Rolf landed someplace where he continued to age. Someplace like right here.

"It's good to see you, Grandfather," Rocket says hopefully.

"Yes, I expect it is," Rolf says, now speaking

in the English tongue. "Took you long enough to get here. When did I send you on your way? Sometime last September?"

What Rolf means by the word *here* is his small dwelling—I believe humans call them trailers— in the middle of a stand of trees behind a large building with signs that proclaim journeyers have found the "Cabazon Casino!"

We are outside a place called Indio, according to the road markers.

"Date?" Rolf says, tossing a piece of fruit in Rocket's direction. It bounces off his chest and lands on the ground, where the Weeping Bat sweeps it up with her mouth.

"It's getting harder and harder out there now, Grandfather. It's getting harder to find vegetable fuels for our engines, and with all the quarantines and permits you need now just to move and gather—"

Rolf waves his hand at his grandson, with a *skut*-like gesture of contempt. "I'm not interested in how you failed." He walks over to my cage and stares more closely at me. "So, my alien friend. Come back to claim that *sklaan* of yours, eh? Oh yes, we kept your objects. Along with files on you. And all your friends."

"We? Who?" I ask.

I get a *skut*-like ignoring as well.

Rolf turns back to his eggling, Rocket. "Yet the very fact you could bring me someone like this lizard makes me hold you in slightly less contempt, Augustus."

"It's Rocket, Grandfather."

"But only slightly less. Did you get any of the things I actually asked for?"

"Yes."

"You used the keys and the pass I supplied to get into the Sandses' lab?"

"Yes."

"And the abandoned equipment was there?"

"Yes."

"'Yes.' Always 'yes.'" Rolf spits on the ground. "You'd say anything to please me. Come inside and let me see for myself. As for all your orphans"—

and now he's waving his hand at us, but again, it seems to be the opposite of a greeting—"they can stay outside."

"Some creatures," I say to Silver Eye, "never get their *laan-tandan*, their life force, unstuck. It seems to wither in them. Of all creatures I know of in different time folds, on different worlds, human mammals seem particularly susceptible. That human creature"—I nod toward the trailer where Rolf and Rocket have disappeared—"that grandsire, in particular. I have met him before. When he was barely older than a hatchling. And by then, something called the Reich had already withered his *laan-tandan* completely."

Yes, there is a deep coldness, a bottomless hard place, inside Grandfather Rolf. In Rocket, though, there is mostly sadness. No one in that family was able to form a healthy pack.

"What transpired?"

I don't know much. Rolf came here after a great war between the humans. Humans have these concepts called "winning" and "losing." Rolf's side lost that war, and yet in the land here, the formation that humans call "America," they still used Rolf's knowledge for "secret" programs of their own. To maximize their power. More strange human concepts.

"Secret programs? Of study?"

Of ways to make weapons that would allow one to hold on to power for eternity. Yet no power lasts that long, and as for secrets, everything, everyplace is known somewhere, somehow, by something. And every being who tastes flesh at the height of their own power eventually falls and turns to dust themselves.

"Tell me again how humans became the dominant mammals on Earth Orange, instead of wolves."

I am not sure. Perhaps wolves were happy with themselves the way they were. That alone makes you unfit to grasp for additional power. I believe Rocket is the direct victim of such grasping. His parents were lost in one of the experiments Rolf carried out for their government. The ideas behind these experiments seem quite strange—the humans attempting to move, control, and change the structure of time and space and of the smallest pieces of matter in the universe, the very bits that make up their own flesh.

"So where we are now, this trailer—this is one of their seats of government? Another lab for experimentation?"

No. This is where Grandfather Rolf lives now. He is a gardener for the human tribe that lives here. They call themselves Morongo, and to survive, they provide gambling and games of chance for the light-skins. Rolf takes care of these trees here. They yield a type of fruit called dates.

"Have you heard of a place called Peenemünde?"

What's that?

"A terrible place, created by a group called the Third Reich. Rolf worked for them before he was brought here. Human mammals enslaved others of their species, forcing them to build machines to kill even more of their kind. I would hope that they are not allowing Rolf to make more Peenemündes here in Eli's—"

KA-BOOM!

One side of the small trailer has just blown out, sending shreds of dirty clothing, decomposing food scraps, and numerous metal containers with the word BEER on the side flying through the air, over the date trees.

"I knew it! I knew it!" the Bearded Boy screams. He had been hiding under my cage the whole time, and now he tries to climb in with me. The Weeping Bat flies overhead, crying, and Rocket comes running out of the burning trailer.

"No, Grandfather! No, I won't let you do it!"

"I only have one WOMPER left!" Rolf screams back at him. "Give me that shielding!"

"No!"

"You took it from the lab for me!"

"Not for this!"

Rolf, for all the *snggg-tlln* his anger gives him, cannot catch up with Rocket. They are running through the woods, and in his frustration, Rolf even tries throwing dates at Rocket, but they merely bounce off him.

Strong Bess staggers up, waving her arms in front of her. "Smoke . . ." she says.

She keeps the hair on her head short, groomed into small spikes, but it is spikier now since she's been singed in whatever conflagration took place in Rolf's trailer. Her face has been badly burned.

"Trying to protect . . . Rocket. . . . Stood in the back, to listen. . . ." She pants. "The world . . . trying to blow up the world. . . . Can't see . . . very well. . . ."

Yes . . . In all the commotion, Silver Eye is able to sort through—to "hear"—many of the panicked thoughts in the air. *Rocket is afraid his grandfather will somehow blow up the world with a WOMPER. . . .*

What the humans call a Wide Orbital Massless Particle Reverser. A highly unstable particle. The very particle trapped in the crystals used by Hypatia and Sacagawea. And Sandusky, Eli's nest-sire, used them in his original time experiments. Rolf must be experimenting here, too, but his trailer hardly seems as if it could house the necessary lab equipment.

. . . *afraid an unstoppable time reaction will swallow the whole world.*

"I have heard legends about such things," I explain to Silver Eye and Bess. "We have a story about the Saurian world Aniok, once considered the most advanced of the Saurian planets, that vanished when they tried experiments to slow down the effects of time's passage on their entire world—"

The humans have a similar story about an island called Atlantis—

"Not the whole world!" Rocket yells. He's run back toward our cages, with Rolf chasing behind him. "I didn't agree to that!"

"You agree to whatever I say you'll agree to!" Rolf shouts. He runs back into his trailer, then emerges a few moments later with one of the favorite implements of human mammals: a gun. "I will use this if I have to."

"Even you couldn't bring yourself to shoot me, Grandfather."

Rolf takes a few steps closer, looks at Rocket.

"Don't be so sure." Then he swivels and aims his gun at Silver Eye. "But I could certainly shoot this dog of yours. No more circus without a mind-reading dog, eh?"

Cages are such a bad idea. Silver Eye is pacing, nervous.

"Don't do it, Grandfather."

I hear weeping, but it's the Bearded Boy crying, not the bat, who's flying overhead.

"Don't do it."

Rolf's finger starts to slowly squeeze the trigger.

"Don't!" And then Rocket takes a parcel out of his jacket, and I can view it clearly. It looks like part of the shielding Sandusky would have used to house decaying particles, containing their own *gerk-skizzy*-ness for a controlled reaction and providing enough positrons in a lab for the WOMPER to constantly charge and then reverse, sending them all moving "backward" in the time stream.

Primitive at best, and certainly too dangerous

to use without rigorous scientific conditions pre-
vailing.

"Time-hopping cannot be done lightly! There
can be bad times to meet!" I say, but it doesn't
help.

Rocket holds out the package. "Here," he says
to his grandsire. "No shooting. No more hurting
anything, or anyone, Grandfather. You're old now.
No more hurting."

"Hurting can be necessary," Rolf hisses.

And just as Rolf is about to grasp the shield
fragment, Rocket throws it in the air — where the
Weeping Bat snatches it. Rolf and Rocket struggle
for the gun, but Rolf seems to remember some
kind of Cacklaw-like battle training from his past
and kicks his grandson in the midsection, briefly
freeing the gun so he can move it —

"No!" The Bearded Boy bursts from under my
cage, where he had been hiding, and tackles
Rolf, who had taken aim at the bat.

But the shot goes off, anyway, and there is a
great *swngll* of wings, as the Weeping Bat is either

hit or startled and drops the shielding to the ground, where it lands on a mound of date-tree branches withering near the remaining three walls of Rolf's trailer.

Panting badly, Rolf performs a high-speed limp to reach the metal fragment before the Bearded Boy can. Rocket gets his wind back and goes after his grandfather, too, but Rolf is able to get to the fragment and sprint-limp, in a *grabaaky* but effective way, back into the trailer, where, through the blasted wall, I can spy a generator and what looks like a crude, unprotected time-sphere apparatus . . .

. . . and it's hard to know what is happening behind the surviving three walls other than to hear Rocket's "No! No! No!" and a long "Owwww!" followed by a high-speed humming and a laugh. And then after that . . .

. . . everything whites out, and I find myself back in the Fifth Dimension, where I really hadn't expected to be at all. At least not for a few more time cycles.

Chapter Twelve

Eli: Huldah

It takes a few minutes for the woman to come over to me. I've brought Thea down a long wet stone staircase—you could barely call them stairs, since going down them was more like reverse rock-climbing in the dark—that led to a large pool, a kind of spring, inside a man-made cave. There's light in here from torches placed into the rocks or held by some of the people who move around in their rough robes and bare feet—it seems a lot of the people here can't even afford sandals.

The woman I'm waiting for wears them,

though. But it's not like she looks rich, or fancy. Her skin, which is already dark, like Thea's, is caked with grime, and her thick, curly black-and-gray hair keeps flopping around as she steps among the piles of straw or rags that pass for mattresses, where all the sick people, the slow pox victims, lie.

Some of them shiver—the way Thea does, shaking against my body. Her shaking has been getting worse. A lot of the people on the straw beds are sweating, twitching, shouting into the air, and even my lingo-spot can't sort out all the screams, though I hear different versions of "God!" and the word *please* a few times, too. And some of the—victims? patients?—just lie quietly, eyes open, but not looking at anything. At least, not anything in this room, or this world. You'd almost think they could see into the Fifth Dimension, they seem to be looking so far away.

The woman has some helpers—other women, some old men, and at least one boy—all of them skinny, like they haven't had enough to eat. They're going around dabbing people's heads, squeezing drops of water on them. But I can't see that anybody here is getting "cured."

One of the patients starts laughing at nothing, and it reminds me of how weird Thea was acting when Mr. Howe and I were in her room in the DARPA tunnels.

Finally, after carefully pouring drops of water down an older woman's throat and patting her forehead with wet rags, the black-and-gray-haired lady walks over to me. She must be the one I'm supposed to see; she seems to be calmer than everyone else around her. She doesn't say anything for a while, just looks at Thea, deep into her eyes, then touches her face.

Thea looks back at the lady and says, "Mermaid." In Hebrew. That was one of Thea's family nicknames, and this woman looks like she could be an aunt of hers or something.

"You're not from anywhere around here, are you?" the woman asks.

"That's one way of putting it," I say. But I can only say it in English. And this woman doesn't have a lingo-spot.

"What a strange tongue. Do you understand mine?"

I nod.

"Then news of this place must have reached you. This was Jerusalem once. The City of David. God's favorite. Or so we thought." She looks around at the people on the straw mounds. One of the sick people again shouts, "Please!" The Healer motions for one of her helpers to go over to the bed and see what's wrong, and the skinny boy runs over. "It's all just ruins now, after all these years of kings—our kings, their kings—and all their wars. But we're the ones left in the ashes. The ones the Babylonians didn't even think were worth taking into slavery. Most of the people you see here were already poor, helpless, hopeless, even before the wars. And because these people were ignored, scorned, that's why our city fell. That's why our king was murdered. Jeremiah told us we'd stopped listening to God."

She sighs and looks around at all the sick people and then at Thea and then at me. "I imagine you're here because you think I can take care of her?"

I nod.

"Is she your wife?"

My face goes so red that I wonder if everyone can see it, even in here, where it's so dark. I mean, I know they got married young back in these old days, but come on.

"The man has stopped shouting now." The boy who'd been helping out has wandered over. "But now he doesn't move at all. Perhaps, Prophet, you should check him."

The woman turns to the boy. "Thank you, Naftali. But you can call me by name. 'Prophet' is a title others gave me. But I am no more favored in the eyes of heaven than you are. Than any of us." She looks around the cave again, then back at me and Thea. She puts her arm around Thea's shoulders and draws her close.

"My name is Huldah. Leave your friend here," she says to me. "I will look after her, though I can't promise anything. This new fever only appeared recently, after the first stranger arrived."

"'First stranger'!" I repeat the words out loud. She must mean A.J.

"Such a strange tongue. But I expect we will come to know what you want. Perhaps you and the stranger are even countrymen. That would make sense. I expect that, because of this, you didn't receive the most hospitable welcome when you arrived. Some people think what the Rebuilder asks is heresy. That it will bring more trouble to us. And with all the leprosies and plagues and invasions, we have had enough trouble. Lead him out of here, Naftali," Huldah tells the boy, and then, looking at me with fierce eyes that also remind me of Thea, says, "I will send for you when we know something."

She takes Thea toward one of the empty piles of straw. "Wait," I say, but she doesn't hear me.

"Seraphic plague," the boy says.

"What?" I say back in English. He looks at me, but is able to figure out the question from the look on my face. After all, it's probably the oldest question there is, going back to caveman times.

"Seraphic plague. That's what they call it.

What the Gehenna-marked have. Because it makes people see things that aren't there, like the seraphim."

He can tell I still don't get it. "Seraphim. Angels. From God. It's not that they start to think they *see* angels; it's that they start to think they *are* angels. Even though Gehenna is where they say the dead go. I guess if you have the plague, it's like being caught between life and death. People who have it think they see everything. And then they go crazy, or they die. That's why they're Gehenna-marked. Come on, I'll take you up to the temple ruins and we'll throw rocks."

"Not now." I go over to Thea. "Stay with me," I tell her, so softly I'm pretty sure no one else can hear us. "Please. I can't afford to lose you, too."

I spend the rest of the night and most of the next day by Thea's bedside. I don't even realize I've drifted off to sleep until Naftali shakes me awake. I'm still holding the rag I was using to dab Thea's face. She's still sleeping, but not well.

Huldah's there, too. "You both needed rest,"

she says. "Now I think you need some air. And sunlight. Let Naftali take you."

I nod and stand. And then I wave, even though Thea's still tossing in her sleep. Guess I better leave before I get too corny and blow her a kiss. I let the boy, Naftali, take me by the hand and lead me back up the slippery, rocky stairs.

The boy is crying in my arms. We've thrown rocks and it's getting dark, and it turns out his family was taken away, or maybe even killed, by the soldiers who came through here and burned everything to the ground.

He wants me to comfort him like a parent would, but how can I do that when I'm just an older kid? Maybe I better take him back down to Huldah. But then, how do I know he won't get slow pox, helping out down there? Which leads to a really weird thought: If he's seen so many terrible things in real life, like his family being hurt, then if he got slow pox, or seraph— whatever they call it—and started seeing things that weren't there, could that really be any worse?

Could things sometimes get so bad that you're better off with a sickness that makes you think you're somewhere else?

Naftali pulls his head away from me and wipes his eyes.

"Jeremiah says someday it can all be better again, that the city can be rebuilt, that God will change our fortunes again, but you can't rebuild a family, can you?"

I think of my dad getting lost in his work, trying to rebuild our family, somehow, and I think of my mom, still lost somewhere in the time stream, and I don't have an answer for him.

"The other stranger wants to help rebuild everything right away," he tells me, "but Jeremiah says the time has to be right, or you'll just have the same old problems all over again."

Naftali seems to brighten up, just a little, because he's finally thought of something to do: "I can take you to Jeremiah! Maybe he can understand you better, since he already has a stranger to talk to."

He takes me through what's left of the palace,

where I guess the king lived. Now it's just black-
ened stumps of wood and big tumbled rocks.

Not too far away, we walk past what's left of
the temple. Those are famous ruins. They were
still fighting over them when I was born. Usually
it involved the killing of innocent people. Just
like Naftali's family.

I would see Jerusalem a lot on the Comnet
news, because people thought God was such a
tiny idea you could only think of God as being
specifically Christian or Jewish or Muslim, and
they'd blow something up, or pull a trigger, to
prove it. But I don't remember ever seeing something like this on the news: a giant statue of . . .
a cow, or something, but fallen over, with one of
its horns cracked in pieces on the ground, and a
permanent startled look on its face. Even in the
setting sun, you could see this was one big cow.

"What is that?" I ask. Naftali may not understand the words, but he sees my pointing finger.

"An ox," he tells me. "From the time of King
Solomon."

One big *ox*.

"There were four of them. Huge. Tremendous. All standing back-to-back, holding a gigantic bowl filled with water on their backs. And so huge, so God-size, that we called it the Molten Sea. The priests would use the water to clean themselves. Those of us who were poor would try to use it, too, sometimes just try to collect the water that would splash out, in our hands, or in bowls, so we wouldn't be thirsty." He stands staring at the place where his family tried to get some extra water. "Now everybody's thirsty, I guess."

He shows me the remains of two giant pillars that stood by the front entrance, tells me about the walls where grain was stored for the year, and shows me another place, an altar, where animals were sacrificed.

"People would take one of their best goats, or sheep or oxen, whatever they had, for one of the feasts, like Rosh Hashanah, or Pesach, and they'd have the animals' necks cut, and then the meat would be burned. You were supposed to be giving back to God some of the good things you'd been given." Naftali stops and looks around the ruins. "Nobody tells you how to give back any of the bad things. I guess you're just stuck with those.

"Anyway, it made the priests mad when Jeremiah would come around and say that doing the sacrifice in exactly the right way wasn't really what God wanted. He said it was more important how we treated each other; that was the main test."

We make a wide circle around some of the timbers and stones, and it's almost completely dark now, and with the ground so slippery from the frost, in all this wreckage, I keep tripping and banging my legs.

"Ow!"

"No! Don't go that way!" Naftali says, like he's a little worried for me. "Over there was where the Holy of Holies was supposed to be. That was the room the high priest would go into on Yom Kippur. It was forbidden to everyone else. That was the day all the grownups were supposed to tell their sins, tell everything they did wrong, and what they wanted to do better in the year that was coming.

Maybe that was the way they tried to get rid of the bad things they did. I don't know if it always worked. But the high priest would go in there — in that special room — and say the name of God." His voice gets quieter, almost a whisper. "The *real* name. Not the short versions like Adonai or Yahweh. But the whole long forbidden name that only the high priest is supposed to know. If anyone else says it, they get burned to a crisp."

Then he stops and I nearly bump into him, and there's anger in his voice. "But you think of all the people who got burned up, anyway, when the Babylonians came — and what did they do? They weren't saying the forbidden name of God."

We move in the dark, more slowly, past the less famous ruins. "Over there was a market," Naftali tells me. He's pointing in the dark, so I can't see anything but shadows caused by the light from the few campfires people have made behind the remnants of walls. Everyone's huddled up, trying to keep themselves warm. "People would sell food there — cloth, oil for cooking, or for lamps. Sandals. My father and mother . . ."

He stops and there is a long pause. I can hear the sniffles and sobs he's trying to cover up. I won't try to ask him what the matter is, or even hold him, if he doesn't want me to.

"My father and mother sold things there, too," he says at last, and then he's moving again, and I try to keep up with him in the dark, more by sound now than anything else.

Then ahead I see it: another campfire, the biggest one, nearly a bonfire, flames going high in the sky, and more voices, at least one of them occasionally shouting. I walk behind Naftali toward the fire, tripping a couple of times over pieces of what used to be homes, slipping on the ice, and then climbing up over the rocks that have been piled together the way kids might do it if they wanted to make a fort.

On the other side of the fort, I see Jeremiah again, the one who told that crowd of people to back off and let me get help for Thea. He's yelling at everyone around the fire now, but in his case, it's not quite like he's mad: "This is God's promise: in this place, which you say is in ruins, with no joyous soul in these desolate streets of Jerusalem, with animals roaming free of their husbandmen, in this forlorn place, there will again come the sounds of joy and gladness! The voice of groom and bride, the wail of new-born babe, the voice of those giving praise to God—all will rise! They will bring new offerings to the temple of God, and these new offerings will find favor with the Lord. And the Almighty will restore them to the land, to this land, as in days of old!"

He paces as he speaks, and everyone watches him.

"Amen!" someone shouts. The only someone I know in the whole crowd, someone who also won't be born for another couple thousand years or more: Andrew Jackson Williams.

He's listening to Jeremiah preaching, and he's raising his arms up to the sky, yelling out words and praise in English, while people around him keep sneaking glances over at him, wondering who or what this other stranger really is, not realizing he will be quoting Jeremiah centuries from now, for crowds of people who gather around *him.*

Maybe for Andrew Jackson, this is even a kind of vacation. After all, all he has to do is listen.

"Him," I tell Naftali. "He's the one I need to see." I point to A.J. and Naftali walks with me, already rubbing his hands and holding them out; it's warmer by the fire.

"But these shall be offerings of praise!" Jeremiah keeps yelling. "Not burnt flesh! These shall be covenants of the heart."

"He was always my favorite preacher," A.J. says to me after I come up next to him. He hardly even seems surprised to see me.

"Boy, have I come a long way to find you," I tell him. "And I think you'd better give me some answers. More and more lives are depending on it." I look at his face in the firelight. He looks right back at me, nods a little bit, then points back out into the darkness, toward Jeremiah, who's still pacing at the edge of the light.

"Jeremiah strips everything to the bone and gets down to business. He puts everything that happens right there in front of you, where you can almost touch it, the good and the bad, and then it's up to you which one you take"—A.J. taps his chest, over his heart—"right in here. Where the answer belongs." Then he lets out a big sigh. "Of course, that means you have to have an answer."

"I need to have an answer," I tell him. "I've lost my mom, my dad's almost a prisoner of the government now, I'll never have a chance to grow up like a normal kid, and all I do is move through history watching grownups burn down cities and start wars. And you always seem to be there. Why? Why are you *here*? Did you come back to stop slow pox? And if you did, how were you planning to get back?"

A.J. just watches the fire dance for a moment and doesn't say anything.

"Can you just tell me what's going on, and why my life is so mixed up with yours? And what's with this 'Rebuilder' name, anyway?"

Naftali is watching both our faces like it's a Ping-Pong match. Is Ping-Pong invented yet? At last, A.J. decides to talk.

"I'm still lookin' for some of those answers myself, boy. Never thought I'd find myself back here, livin' out God's word directly in the Bible. Don't know if I'm worthy of bein' in such company. But I don't know anything about this 'Rebuilder' business."

"He's someone who fits your description . . . who suddenly appears in certain editions of the Bible," I tell him. "That's one reason I came back. You seemed to be messing up history even more than it already is. Everyone's scared."

He shakes his head. "Then it's the exact opposite of what I wanted to do," he says. "I just wanted to vanish. But first I wanted to help your father."

"How? Help my father how?"

"Lotsa answers, son. And we either have all the time in the world or it's running out faster than we imagine. I can't tell just yet. But let's try starting at the beginning. The path that hooks both of us together also runs through these two." And then he reaches into his pocket and pulls out an old photograph—not the microchip kind with different scenes or three dimensions on it, but the old flat-paper type with just one picture on it that doesn't move at all.

But this one doesn't need to move to keep my eyeballs focused, to almost knock me out, or at least to surprise me more than stepping into the pages of the Bible to have a talk with A.J. It's a picture of my mom, standing in an old-fashioned dress, from like when Mickey Mantle still played with the Yankees. The kicker is, she's with Rolf Royd, the Dragon Jerk kid, except that he's a Dragon Jerk grownup in this one. And even worse, his arm is around her.

And standing next to them is Andrew Jackson Williams.

Chapter Thirteen

Eli: Uproot and Pull Down

I need to ask A.J. about this picture, need to find out what's been going on with my parents, with my mom, with the whole history of DARPA, but I haven't gotten the chance, since Jeremiah keeps preaching, shouting out, and A.J. is constantly distracted, listening to him.

"When was that picture taken?" I ask. "What was she doing?" I reach for him, but he steers my hand away and points toward the campfire. "Shh, son. In a minute. Jeremiah's catchin' the spirit now."

Apparently "the spirit" makes you yell a lot: "God said to me, I chose you before I created you in the womb! There is no escape for you! The words you are given will hound you till you give them voice—words that will uproot and pull down! Just as He said that our people not only uproot, pull down, and destroy—but eventually replant. And rebuild.

"These are the words, the visions, I've been given. They do not come from me. They come from the Holy Source, from which all life springs. They come from the God we were meant to follow!"

Jeremiah paces around the fire as he talks. It's clear and cold this evening; people pull rags and shawls and pieces of whatever they can find over their shoulders, but it's not enough, and most of them shiver. Most, but not Jeremiah, who has that rough, dirty shawl over his bony body, and a sandal on one cracked and scabby foot.

On the other foot, there's only bare skin, but it's tough and scabby, too, like alligator hide.

Naftali raises his hand, like he's in a classroom.

Once he realizes Jeremiah isn't looking at any-one in particular but gazing out into the dark as he talks, he just asks his question out loud.

"We've been trying to replant, but all this cold weather came. Will God help us?"

"Does God play tricks?" Jeremiah asks in re-turn. In the firelight, his eyes seem even sadder now. "You see the hand of the Almighty all around you. Nothing is hidden; everything that has come to pass is in plain view."

"But what about the food?" someone else asks, nodding toward Naftali.

Jeremiah sighs. "Before we can plant, we need to gather seeds. When this snow passes, you can go to the fields the Babylonians put to the torch. Sweep away the ashes. Gather what survives. Raise it up and let it grow."

"Is this another of God's lessons you're giving us?" a woman asks. She's the one who said Thea was Gehenna-marked.

"No, I'm telling you where to plant crops. This lentil bread should be finished cooking in the fire soon. We will share it when it's ready."

"But then these lentils will be gone!" the woman says.

"Have you forgotten what time of year it is?" Jeremiah says wearily. "It's Rosh Hashanah, the New Year. Time to think of winter crops, not spring. And time to ask forgiveness for what we've done, what we've been. Time to ask for blessings."

"How? With sacrifices? We have no animals, no offerings to take to the temple! We have no more sacrifices to make!" the first man shouts.

"We'll sacrifice you!" the Gehenna-woman shouts at Jeremiah. "You brought on this misery, with all your talk!"

The rest of the crowd shouts their agreement and moves to surround Jeremiah. It isn't just me or A.J. or Thea—anyone can become a "stranger" at a moment's notice, I guess, when everyone is so scared. And if everyone else is scared, it's hard not to be that way yourself—whether it's the middle of war or sickness or just feeling lost and alone. And then you don't think real clearly, and how do you ever change your situation?

I'm working real hard on trying not to be scared right now.

"I just wanted some food," Naftali says in a quiet voice. I think I'm the only one who hears him. Naftali has even more-basic concerns.

A.J. has been tending the bread, or what's called bread. The loaves are like big, thick pancakes, and A.J. reaches into the edge of the fire and rips off a piece.

"Here!" he says, speaking in Hebrew, holding up the piece of bread. "Here is your sacrifice! A piece of the meal we were to share!"

The crowd stops, looks from Jeremiah to A.J. A.J. keeps going. "We'll offer it up to God! We'll ask for every blessing for what we do!"

"We don't have an altar," the Gehenna-woman says. "We don't even have a temple."

A.J. looks around, like maybe they have a point, but then he turns back to the group. "Then we'll make one, right here."

And he sets the bread down, then starts picking up big rocks from the rubble.

Naftali's holding up a torch and following

A.J., so he can see what he's doing, which earns him bites of the lentil loaf A.J. was cooking.

It seems Jeremiah might be saved, for now. Everyone else is standing around watching A.J. work.

I'm helping, too, picking up smaller rocks and carrying them. I'm starting to understand how he got the Rebuilder name. But I also want to talk to A.J., to ask him more about that picture.

Though right now, all he wants to talk about is the temple.

"This was the great temple of the early Israelites, son. People would come from all over the country for all the great holidays, like Passover, and the Jewish New Year."

"Rosh Hashanah?"

"Yeah. They were tribal people, mostly, so they'd bring something to offer up to their god."

"The sacrifices everyone's talking about?"

"Right. Something to let the heavens know you appreciate what you have, and if it wasn't too much trouble, you'd also appreciate not starving to death in the new year, or for no one to get sick, your kids to be taken care of, all the usual things people want. Hand me that rock."

He takes a flat stone I'm holding, then tries to lay it across the other rocks, like a tabletop. He shakes his head. "Too small."

"So, since the temple was destroyed . . ."

". . . they can't talk to God in the ways they're used to. Jeremiah was talkin' about getting blessings for these new crops they want to plant."

"Do hungry people have time for blessings?"

A.J. doesn't answer that. "I need to find some more rocks," he says.

I go with him, and Naftali follows us with the torch.

"I really need to know more about that picture," I tell A.J. "You have me all scared that something happened to my mom."

"She tried to do some good, son. But the story of that picture really begins with our buddy Rolf Royd. He came back from his trip through the Fifth Dimension, showing up somewhere in America, in the 1950s, a few years after World War II. That turned out okay for him, because some of the new government agencies, especially the spy agencies that America had created, decided a few of those Nazis knew things that could still be useful. The German rocket scientists, too — we gave 'em jobs workin' for us."

"Scientists? Like the one Thea and Clyne met in that big cave, with the factory in it?"

"Yeah — Wernher von Braun. Give me a hand lifting this rock up. Yeah, him and other ex-Nazis. But not just building rocket ships. Some of 'em got work with our spy outfits, teaching them what they knew."

"What did they know?"

"How to keep track of people. How to keep your citizens from doin' things you don't want 'em to do. It was called Operation Paperclip. Hey, this one look big enough to you?"

It's flat enough and big enough to go between those other stones he set up. But it looks heavy. Still, if I help him, it keeps him here, and keeps him talking. "I think so."

"Then help me take it over there." He grunts a bit but continues his story without me asking.

Maybe to take his mind off how heavy the rock is. "Yeah, Operation Paperclip. We took those Nazis right into our own government because we thought another big war was brewin', with the Russians." He shakes his head. "Nobody can really think straight during a war."

No kidding. During World War II, there was another secret project we both knew about: Project Split Second—the time-travel research my mom was working on with Samuel Gravlox and his team in San Francisco. She tried to slow the work down, so that time travel wouldn't be invented too soon and turned into some kind of weapon that might mess up the world even more.

"After the explosion at Fort Point, which you were part of, they moved their operations to a secret base in the Oklahoma panhandle," A.J. explains, moving slowly with me as we keep dragging the rock. "Just like the work on atomic bombs, they didn't slow down their time-travel research just because one war was over. The idea was, the next war would be even more fierce, more destructive." He shakes his head again.

"Your mother stayed on the Split Second team, Eli. She tried to be a voice of reason. That's what got her in trouble."

"'Trouble'?"

"Accused of being a peacenik, a communist, a spy. Whatever they could accuse her of, because she wanted everyone to think twice about the kinds of weapons we were buildin'. But they had somebody else who knew about time travel, knew how it could work. Someone they decided could run the Split Second team, since they were havin' doubts about your mom."

There was a sick feeling in my stomach, like what happens if you eat donuts and ice cream and a big jug of soda pop, all at once. "Rolf?"

A.J. just nods.

"He worked with my mom?"

"Yeah, after the war. He was part of what they called the 'team.' His hair was stark white, even though he was still supposed to be a young man."

"He really worked with her?"

"He worked with everybody. Anybody that could make him more powerful. All the way through the 1960s."

"So she's definitely still alive." I don't ask it as a question. I was always too scared to ask the question. Now I'm just relieved.

"Ready? Heave!" We lift the flat rock and let it crash down on the two big stones A.J. has set up. It stays put, and we have our table.

"Altar. It's done, son. The first part of re-buildin' the temple for these people." A.J. wipes off his hands and looks at me. "Maybe things can get back to normal now. As for your mom . . ."

"She's alive, but you haven't told me where."

"She *was* alive, certainly back then. But I've lost track of her." My stomach gets all queasy again. "That doesn't mean anything bad's happened to her! I just wasn't always able to keep tabs, since I had some of my own problems with Rolf, and with our fine government folk to contend with."

"Don't lie to me. I'm sick and tired of grownups lying to me."

Now he puts his hands on my shoulders and stares at me, straight in the eye. His own eyes don't quite seem as crazy anymore—just sort of unknowable, like really deep pools. "I ain't never, ever gonna lie to you, son. That's one piece of reality you can hang on to forever. And listen, I got a couple more secrets for you to keep. Here's the first one." He hands me something, wrapped in paper torn from a book.

People have already been watching us since we've been "rebuilding" part of the temple, trying to understand the English we've been speaking the whole time. Now they see the small item he's about to pass me.

Even Jeremiah, who's been sitting, still surrounded by people, waiting to see how this is all going to turn out. There's enough firelight to let me see his eyes widen.

"Maybe later." A.J. quickly stuffs it back in his pocket, but not before I can see what it is: a small piece of mirror with a little ceramic frame around it, one of those gifts they were giving away at the Fairmont Hotel, where my mom lived when she was in San Francisco. From that old-time radio show *One Man's Family*: "You are reflected in your friends, family, and times! *One Man's Family* on NBC Radio."

"Glass hasn't been invented yet, let alone mirrors. It would startle 'em," he whispers. "But I was gonna leave it here, as the first offerin' on the altar."

"I think you already have left it."

"What do you mean, son?"

"Someone in the future finds the mirror here, when they're digging around. They even find traces of you."

"Me?"

"In new versions of the Bible that start cropping up. You're called 'the Rebuilder.'"

"Really? The name sticks even in the holy writ? That just seems wrong, boy, if they're talkin' about me. I just said a few words, is all, about not givin' up the ship. Talked about the need to rebuild. Pretty humble helpin' hand, in the scheme of things."

"Are you both magic?" Naftali asks us. He's been watching us the whole time and noticed the firelight the mirror bounced on my face. "Where did you *really* come from?"

But before A.J. or I can answer the question, there's a huge explosion—the kind that comes from time-traveling.

People scream and scatter.

I hear one voice I recognize: "A good time to meet?"

See several faces I don't.

And at least one—straight out of the picture A.J. showed me—that I'd hoped never to see again.

Chapter Fourteen

Thea: Wakenings

583 B.C.E.

This time, I know I'm not dreaming. I see the face of a woman, who introduces herself as Huldah, leaning over me. I'm in a cave, lit by torches. From the sounds I hear, and what I can see when I lift my head, this is an infirmary.

Have I been sick?

I know I've had vivid dreams—all the way back to when I was with Sally Hemings, the Ethiopian princess, in the time of Jefferson President. So many strange things have happened since then—I spoke with a horse; we discovered the bones of a slave girl named Brassy, who was important in ways no one knew about; Eli and I discovered we'd each had birth anniversaries while time-voyaging, and we even kissed each—

Kissed?

All of this occurred after it first seemed the lingo-spot was speaking in a voice of its own. I know we came back to Eli's time, then were taken captive by his government, though that feels dreamy, too, especially memories of a birth-day party that Eli and his father and Mr. Howe held in my room.

"You aren't dreaming."

It's the woman who just introduced herself as Huldah. She's the healer here, I believe. She re-acts to the look on my face. I don't even need the lingo-spot to understand her. She speaks in one of the local tongues, the language of the Hebrews.

"When you were feverish, you spoke out loud about dreams, about your friend Eli."

My face must be showing even more surprise.

"Most people with the fever you had imagine visions, phantoms, people who aren't there. Eli was here. But he has left with Naftali. It is often easier for people to let us tend their loved ones when they don't have to watch their agony. In any event, you aren't dreaming."

Loved ones? "I . . . had it, then? The slow pox?"

"Seraphic plague. Many people don't come back from it. However, we discovered the waters down here can be beneficial. At first you didn't seem to respond to our cure. Then finally, your fever broke."

How strange that I never came down with the pox during any of the outbreaks in Alexandria— that I had to move centuries away from home to become its victim. Perhaps it is a different form of the illness that I became vulnerable to. Whatever form, words seem to come with some difficulty when I try to speak.

"You can . . . cure the pox? Mother was only able to reduce the s-s—the symptoms—she never could treat it . . . compl—"

My tongue suddenly seems stuck in my mouth, and I am aware of how much larger than normal it feels. I motion to my mouth.

Huldah nods, then picks up a cup from the ground. "Yes, pox sufferers need to keep wet inside. The body must stay supple."

"A cure?" I ask again after I've sipped.

"The waters here in the pond, from the *wadi*"—*wadi,* the old familiar word for *river*—"it brings some of the sufferers back to themselves after a few days."

"How did you learn this?"

"I discovered it when I first came down here myself. I was also suffering from the fever. This was shortly after the Babylonians burned our city. Wanderers and strangers came to pick through the ruins. And shortly after, the one called the Rebuilder came. Not to loot the rubble, but to tell us Jeremiah was still right. A new city could rise in this place, if we wanted it. But it has been hard for so many broken hearts to place much faith in such an idea.

"At first it was hard to know if I was ill; when you are a 'prophet,' you already suffer a number of unwelcome voices in your head, so sometimes it is hard to tell if you are ailing in the usual way."

I knew of prophets in Alexandria. "Voices from the gods?" I ask.

"Not only God. To be a prophet is to hear everyone's voice. Everyone's suffering. That's what makes the task so difficult." Huldah turns away. "And the fever made it unbearable, especially with all the suffering Jerusalem has seen. When I took ill, I came down here to remove myself from the world above . . . and let the seraphim take me. It seems the heavens had something else in mind for me, however, in this world below the city."

"What happens when you go back above?" I look around the large cavern and try to remember my own fever dreams of arriving in Jerusalem with Eli, to remember what the world looked like above us.

"That's the one thing the waters couldn't cure," Huldah tells me. "I still haven't been able to go back above to our city of David. I still cannot bear to see it, or see the conditions of those who can barely be called survivors."

"But don't they need you up there as well?"

"My work now is to stay down here and do what I can."

I sip water for a few moments before speaking again.

"I can see that being a prophet isn't such an easy task. Especially now in . . . Yerushalayim." I sound out the name slowly, as more of my fever dreams come back to me.

"Yes. Or what's left of it. There's no place left to send you, now that you've healed."

"You remind me of my mother," I tell her, using the Hebrew tongue as best I can.

"Your mother? I suspect I am old enough to be your grandmother. At least."

I try to rise up from my sleeping mound, but my body is stiff—my back, my legs.

"That's usually what happens when the fever leaves—the limbs are fatigued. You'll have a hard time moving for a while. But still, you are lucky. Better to rest."

One of the men sleeping near me begins screaming, "No, I did not! *No I did not go to Gehenna!*" Yelling to no one in particular, he then just as suddenly lapses into a wide-eyed, shivering silence.

Gehenna.

"I was . . . Gehenna-marked?" I ask. I'm not sure what it means, but I recall that someone accused me of that recently.

"I don't let them use that phrase here. Gehenna is one of the valleys where the dead are said to dwell. To be 'Gehenna-marked' is to have no hope of recovery. But you, and others, have proven them wrong." The way she talks, she seems deeply sad, the way Mother did in those last weeks before Alexandria burned, when the civil war had broken out and people were attacking one another on the streets.

The shivering man starts yelling again.

"Excuse me." Huldah, with her Mother-like smile that isn't quite a smile, turns to walk over to him.

"Wait," I say, but she doesn't hear; she's given her attention to the man.

One of the women who is helping her—it is hard to tell the difference between those who are well and those who are ailing in a place like this, as both are underfed and dressed in rags, with scars and wounds—goes over to the man after scooping out some hot broth from a bubbling kettle nearby.

I swing my legs off the straw pad, and though they hurt, I set them down on the floor.

I can't quite sense the ground under my feet—my legs feel as if sword tips are jabbing them, over and over, while my feet feel as though they've spent too much time in cold water and have a kind of numbness about them.

I try to stand, but instead fall down.

Huldah turns from the shivering man to help me. "Really, you should rest, young friend," she says as she lifts me back up.

She doesn't even know my name. "Thea. My name is Thea."

"Thee-ah?" It is good, a comfort, to hear her pronounce it. "Thea, if I may say, while plague sufferers are known to hear different voices and have visions while in the grip of fever, I have never known any of them to use as many different voices as you did while you were in its throes. So many voices, Thea. Has anyone ever suggested that you, too, might be a—"

She doesn't get to finish. From the opening of the tunnel, on top of the rough stairs carved out of these rocks, comes the sudden, though distant *boom* of an explosion.

That explosion is followed by shouting and terrified screams, as explosions usually are.

Whatever color is left in Huldah's face drains away. "No. Not more Babylonians," she whispers. "There is nothing in Jerusalem left to destroy."

Eli. Where is Eli?

"Did you say my friend was up there?" I ask.

"Yes—"

I try to jump off the sleeping mound but still meet difficulty as my legs buckle underneath me. I pull myself up and start to move toward the stairs, wobbly as I am.

With the sound of the explosion, more people in the room have been groaning, yelling about their fever dreams.

"I can't lose . . . my friend," I tell her. "We are . . . all we have left."

"But you can't . . ."

But I do, even though I fall to one knee—twice, each time a different knee, and each time it hurts—while trying to walk with prickly, numb legs.

"Go with her." Huldah motions to the woman who's been helping her with the screaming man, and she comes over and puts my arm around her shoulder, and we move forward—haltingly, but forward. She's emaciated and looks haunted, too. Seeing her face in the torchlight makes me wonder which one of us should be supporting the other up the stairs.

On our slow, steady way up—I slip only once and bang my shin instead of a knee—I learn that her name is Yehudit and that she's not much older than I am but already has a husband and a child, both of whom were taken by the Babylonians.

"They want slaves and workers," she says, "everybody working to make their empire bigger."

She tells me the invasions came about when Israel's king, Zedekiah, refused to keep paying ransom money to the Babylonian king, Nebuchadnezzar. "As we were once warned," Yehudit says, "kings get to decide, and we suffer."

"Maybe you'll get to see your family again," I tell her, to be helpful. At least they weren't murdered, like my mother was. And they are all still living in the same time, which makes a reunion somewhat possible.

"That's what keeps me alive," she replies. "That's my hope."

But then it also strikes me how no one is really left alone by history. It swallows us up when all we want to do is share a meal with someone we love or sit about on a warm afternoon with a friend.

We're at the top of the stairway. It's dark outside, but we can see shadows moving about.

"I'm not going out there," Yehudit tells me. "If it's more Babylonians, I don't want to know. I can't."

"You'll be all right," I tell her.

What makes me suddenly reassure her? It's almost as though a lingo-spot voice were telling me, a voice from outside—and yet from inside at the same time. As if my own thoughts and the voices heard by the lingo-spot are merging together, becoming one.

A great quantity of voices and thoughts, all channeled through me.

I'm not sure I like the idea. But perhaps I'm wrong. I should ask Huldah about this. About how you protect yourself when it seems your eyes and ears are open to the whole wide world. "The people outside aren't Babylonians," I reassure Yehudit.

And I know *exactly* where that knowledge comes from: one of the voices is carrying in the night air.

"A good time to meet?"

It's K'lion. Yerushalayim *has* been invaded again, but not by soldiers. By time travelers.

Chapter Fifteen

Clyne: Nerve Tissue

583 B.C.E.

Uncontrolled time reactions inevitably lead to uncontrolled results, a spacetime flow as *gerk-skizzy* as the faultiest ship's drive. Couple such unstructured time-roaming with the innate unpredictability and hot-bloodedness of mammals themselves, and you have a grid of random probabilities to challenge the wiliest mathematician.

You may try to calculate, but in fact, you never know where you'll wind up or who you'll be with. As a result of Eli's earlier extemporaneous time leap, he became a passenger in my ship, and cause and effect being the quantum, often unknowable things they are, I have, ever since, found myself stranded here on Earth Orange.

Not that I regret the experience. The mere idea that mammals are capable of advanced evolution is worth several Saurian life cycles of study. And never mind what one learns being an outlaw.

However, Rolf's uncontrolled time reaction, undertaken in his trailer with a WOMPER he had secreted from the government agencies on Eli's planet, did not turn out so happily.

Several of us who should have made the trip are missing: the Weeping Bat, Strong Bess — and Silver Eye. I have arrived here in the company of Rocket Royd, who appears to be passed out, along with the Bearded Boy, who doesn't . . . and Rolf, who is wide awake and trying to make his own kind of sense of what just happened.

But happily, wherever we are, and whatever *has* just happened, I believe I see Eli by one of the campfires.

"A good time to meet?" I venture.

The only answer I get is a projectile thrown past my ear, and the words "Goat-demon!" shouted in my direction. *Goat?*

"The demon gods are here!"

"You did this, Jeremiah! You brought this on us, with all your doom and gloom!"

Most of the people are running away. A couple run toward us.

"Eli! Watch out!" Thea's voice. She's here, too! The ruined rock buildings make me think we are in her time. Good. She can explain, perhaps, that I am not a demon god. Or a goat. If we get the chance.

"A good time to meet? Or not?" I say in Thea's tongue.

"Clyne!" Eli's voice. He is definitely here. But he's in a small group being surrounded, near the fire.

"This isn't Jeremiah's doin'." It's the distinct mammalian dialect of the one named A.J. We're all here. At this place. At this time.

Perhaps one result of all these time reactions and chronological leaps is becoming predictable—

at least enough for me to refine a hypothesis: time travel disrupts the flow of "history" enough that a new prime nexus is created wherever a time voyager lands. If Eli or A.J. were here first, their very presence would be enough to draw, to attract, other chronological explorers, like waves circling a whirlpool. At least here on Earth Orange, the interconnections created by the plasmechanical material that's been loosed upon this planet only exacerbate the effects.

"No, no, no!" A mammal boy, younger than Eli, begins kicking me.

"No more, no more, no more! Go back!" It doesn't even occur to me to try a slaversaur roar with one so young. "No more! There's no one left to take! There's no one left to hurt! Go back, go back! We don't want you Babylonians!"

"But I am a Saurian," I tell the hatchling.

"Then go back to Saronia!" the boy yells.

"It would be Saurius Prime, and I believe for now I am str—" But the boy is too upset, and he picks up a projectile, some bit of discarded mineral material, and throws it at me.

I move my head and the object misses, but it grazes Rocket, who is just waking up and now yells, "Ow!" very loudly and starts rubbing his head. Then he starts to look around, and then his mouth starts to move, but it's a while before anything audible comes out. And when it does, the syllables sound a small and squeaky *klnny,* then all he manages is, "Uh-oh." He's never time-voyaged before. "What has Grandfather done now? Grandfather!" He is wobbly getting to his feet. "What have you done!?"

But Rolf doesn't answer. True to character, he has used all the mammalian skirmishing to slip away.

But it wasn't Rolf that brought us here. Not really. True, he initiated the reaction. But I believe what brought us here, as the evidence supporting my hypothesis grows stronger, was the sentient plasmechanical material from Saurius Prime, which is steadily mutating here in this mammalian dimension. I believe it has been fusing with the properties of the slow pox DNA to make a neural network, a kind of nerve tissue not just connecting separate human beings, but separate times as well.

"Ow, hatchling!" The young mammal has given up throwing objects and returned to the more reliable close-quarter fighting method of kicking.

"Stop! Stop it!" It's the Bearded Boy, James, who comes over and puts himself between the hatchling and me. "He's not going to hurt you." But I'm not sure which one of us he's talking to, since this angry young mammal can't understand James's words. Though his hand gestures should be eminently readable.

"No," James says to the other boy. James's resiliency surprises me. In what little light there is — besides the nearby fires, the sun is just now breaking over the horizon — I believe he sees the surprise on my face.

"When I was on the street," he says to me, "I would be kicked or hit for how I looked. I don't know where we are now or how we got here, but that kind of hurting has got to stop.

"No," the Bearded Boy tells the angry hatchling again. But then, even in the dim light of the nearby fires and the early sunrise, he must see something familiar in the young mammal's face or in his eyes, because then he adds, "Please."

"Naftali!" Eli shouts at the hatchling. "He won't hurt you." Like the Bearded Boy, Eli is speaking the English of his people. And despite the way plasmechanical material is using all of us to spread itself around, I don't believe this young boy is wearing a lingo-spot. I hope he is as adept at reading expressions as I believe him to be.

"Excuse me," I tell the hatchling. Then I pick him up—I hope he's never seen *Slaversaur!*—and set him down closer to James. "You two should be open-palmed trust colleagues," I tell him, using Thea's tongue. I hope it is close enough. I haven't been here long enough to fully understand the local idiom. "You could protect each other." I repeat it in both their languages.

"We are in a period of uncontrolled time reactions, and young ones are especially vulnerable."

With that, I hop over to see if I can help Eli. Somebody's always after that boy, and he doesn't even look like a dinosaur.

Chapter Sixteen

Eli: Wrestling with Angels

We're all under some kind of house arrest. On top of that, A.J.'s bleeding from a head wound, Thea seems better but is still weak, and Rolf Royd, the Dragon Jerk Kid—who didn't look so much like a kid anymore when he arrived in a time explosion early this morning—is running around loose somewhere in Biblical Jerusalem, causing who-knows-what kind of damage to history itself. But all of us, especially Clyne and Jeremiah, are guarded now, surrounded, not allowed to take more than one or two steps.

Apparently, from what I can pick up from Thea, Jeremiah himself, and the snatches of conversation translated by the lingo-spot, the people here are deciding whether to stone Jeremiah to death, since they blame him for many of their misfortunes.

The arrival of Clyne — and the remnants of the carnival that he'd been with — was the last straw. The survivors here are sick and tired and at the ends of their ropes, with nothing left to lose. There was all that talk about rebuilding and sacrifice. But I guess too many people think that that will take too long and that it would be faster and easier to kill us — and it might be worth finding out if that makes God happier. The woman who keeps talking about Gehenna brought it up. "Your words," she said to Jeremiah, "your words said all this would happen. They *made* it happen."

"If only my words had such power," Jeremiah sighed. That's when they took their spears and knives and rocks and put us here, in the middle of what used to be their temple, right next to the altar A.J. and I were building.

"This isn't exactly what I had in mind when I talked about makin' offers to God," A.J. whispered to me at one point. "I didn't mean us." This was after he'd already been hurt—one of the flying rocks hit him in the head during the growing hysteria about the new arrivals.

Jeremiah holds his hands over the ashes remaining from the fire, then puts them together when he realizes there's no heat left. "The summer is past," he says. "The harvest is come, and we are not saved."

A.J. groans and rubs his head.

"Getting rid of me will not free them of their burdens." Jeremiah turns to A.J. "When you came here, I was prepared to vanish from Jerusalem, where I was no longer wanted and where the sight of me reminded everyone—man, woman, and child—of their unending sorrows. When I was ready to vanish, it was you who told me to stay. Told me that things could yet be made whole, made right. You wanted to start rebuilding, even then, holding on to a simple faith that even I was in danger of losing."

While that sounds good, I'm remembering what Thirty and Mr. Howe were saying before I left, about all the sudden changes in Biblical history, and maybe Jeremiah isn't supposed to stay — maybe that's one of the "breaks" in history we have to try to fix.

But now that Thea's here, and seems to be cured, part of me wants to just put on my cap and go with her and Clyne and maybe A.J. But I already know I can't leave Rolf here, and on top of that, if something happens to Jeremiah that wasn't supposed to . . . well, we have to keep history from getting even more messed up than it already is.

Besides Thea feeling better, the only other bright spot right now is that Naftali seems to have become friends with the kid that Clyne brought with him — James, the Bearded Boy. He looks a little bit like a small Bigfoot, I guess, with fur all over his body.

He's sort of cute. Thea seems to think so, too. She's been translating for Naftali and James, so they can understand each other. They've both discovered that neither of them has any parents around.

"Friend Eli," Clyne whispers to me now.

"Yes?"

"What is the custom here with this kind of *snnkt!* legal proceeding? When do we find out whether they will stone us?"

"I'm not sure. I never read the Bible much. And even though these people are in the stories"— I point to Jeremiah and the people surrounding us—"you and I and everybody else with us sure aren't. So we're in the middle of a brand-new story that hasn't ended yet."

"Can't that be said about all *fnnntk!* lives? And stories? And what is this Bible?"

"It's a very powerful collection of stories for humans who are Jewish or Christian. Belief systems about the way the world was created. About how to act toward other humans, about what God wants us to do."

"'God' . . . is the mammalian name for *skkt!* the *Endu-kaan*?"

"I don't know, Clyne. What is the *Endu-kaan*?"

"Melonokus called the *Endu-kaan* 'the great source of all *thmmb-skizzles.*'"

"I'm not sure that helps." I look out at the crowd. They're talking to one another, pointing back at us. I pick up stray words that don't comfort me, like *rid,* and *stone.* I keep watch out of the corner of my eye, then turn back to Clyne, stepping in front of him so it's a little harder for the people around us to see him.

"A *thmmb-skizzle* is what feeds . . . your spirit, what sparks your life. Melonokus wrote, during the Bloody Tendon Wars, that there was no *snnnt!* reason for us to keep eating each other. 'Nothing compares to the nourishment of the *Endu-kaan,* so wipe that blood off your face,' he said. According to the legends."

"Maybe it's something like that. But I never really went to church or synagogue much. Except sometimes for Christmas or maybe a friend's bar mitzvah."

"Were you of these Jewish or Christian *thmmb-skizzle* groups?" Clyne asks.

"Both, really. I had grandparents who were

both. Parents who were at least a little of both."

"But there are many such *thmmb-skizzle* groups on Earth Orange?"

"Yes," I tell him. "They're all called religions. Not just Jewish or Christian, either. Muslims, and people who believe in Buddha, and the ones in India . . ."

"*Tkkknt!* Hindus?" Clyne says.

"Yes! How did you know?"

"I recall a travel-entertainment shown on your Comnet, between dinosaur movies. This India was mentioned."

I've known Clyne for centuries, in a way. But I realize I don't have nearly as good a memory as he does.

"And each *thmmb-skizzle* group claims to believe in God?" he asks.

"Each group has a different name for God, but in the end, it's still God. And sometimes there are more than one."

"Each often willing to *zkkkt!* kill the other

groups over what they insist is the essential goodness of *their* gods?"

"Yeah. Usually."

"That doesn't seem very *thmmb-skizzly.*"

"I know."

"So this Jeremiah we are detained with . . ."

"He's what they call a 'prophet,'" I tell him.

"What are they?"

"As near as I can figure, they go around telling people to treat each other better, and everyone winds up hating them for it."

"Melonokus had similar *szzzn!* experiences," Clyne says.

"But then later, people act like they agreed with them all along, like they just want to be lovey-dovey, too. Even when it's not true. Did that happen to Melonokus?"

I step a little closer to Clyne—whether to protect him or just to shut out the crowd a moment or two longer, I'm not sure. I look at Thea, and she seems to be doing the same thing with the two littler kids, just drawing them close. Clyne, as usual, seems more excited than scared.

"We are required to read *Jail Notes of a Bad Lizard* in school now. There is little mention that once, before the Bloody Tendon Wars had *sknnnt!* ended, mere possession of the writings was enough to earn a jail sentence of one's own. But in that volume"—and if it's possible to describe a dinosaur face as "brightening up," I'd say Clyne suddenly looks like he's seen a report card with all A's—"Melonokus notes that the hardest prisons to leave are the ones we build ourselves, *szzlp!*, in here." And Clyne taps the right side of his chest, where I guess his heart is. "Although we also seem to spend far too much time detained by *zgggt!* authorities here on your world."

Jeremiah has been watching us. "And what messages do strangers bear in a time when few are ready to listen?" he asks.

"He's been making plans with the goat-demon!" one of our guards shouts. There's no more shutting out the crowd anymore; another couple of rocks come whizzing by.

Then Clyne turns to Jeremiah and repeats the

last part of what he just said, about the hardest prisons being the ones you keep yourself locked up in, inside. But now he says it in Hebrew.

Jeremiah nods. Slowly, and then a little faster. "How strange that I should find myself sharing thoughts with a goat-demon. I have been thrown in stocks and left in prison, too. But I have so far kept the jailers out of here." He taps his own heart—on the left side—then turns toward the crowd surrounding us.

"These people are innocent!" He points to us. "None deserve to be held by you! They are strangers who have come to us in their time of need! Even if it is *our* time of great need as well! Who is to say this is not part of God's plan, too?" He stands by the cold remains of the fire. "If it is me you blame for the presence of the goat-demon," he says as he points to Clyne, "blame me as you will! Though this demon, perhaps born horribly deformed—"

"I was a good egg," Clyne says a little indignantly.

"—is likewise merely a stranger, who comes

to us asking for help. We talked before of helping ourselves — planting crops for the new year, even though our numbers are small. I then said we needed to make blessings, here, where the temple stood, to ask for a good new year. A year that will sustain and nourish and not brutalize us. But the Rebuilder and his friends have helped me see — we need to rebuild *here* first" — and Jeremiah taps his chest again, this time so everyone else can see it — "before we start raising walls again. We carry the temple, and all it stood for, inside us now. We each have these seeds, and we each tend the crop that's been given us. Yes, the harvest is past, the summer is gone, and we were not saved. But there comes another time to plant and reap. Right now, the sun has returned, and the frost is melting. I am no longer content to stay in these ruins. I have *new* planting to do." Jeremiah walks toward the edge of the circle. Thea — and the guy named Rocket, who is apparently related to Rolf — move to let him by.

Jeremiah passes us and keeps walking into

the crowd of people holding the rocks and sticks. No one stops him.

"We haven't decided your fate yet," the Gehenna-woman says.

"My fate is not for you to decide," he replies. He then puts his hands on two of the crude spears and pushes them aside. Jeremiah stands his ground, as everyone else shifts on their feet, wondering what to do, wondering whether they should hurt the prophet or let him walk away.

"Egypt," A.J. whispers.

"What?" I ask.

"If he goes, he'll keep walkin' straight to Egypt, after he's done plantin'. Jeremiah just disappears from the Bible completely, once he leaves Jerusalem. We gotta stop him." Maybe it was the bonk on the head that's keeping him from thinking clearly. It's also keeping him from moving too fast, so when he goes after Jeremiah, I catch up quickly and put my arm around his shoulders.

"A.J., no, you can't."

"Why not?"

First off, there's no reason to believe that those people will let us walk past the spears the way Jeremiah just did. But there's an even bigger reason I have to stop A.J. "If he's supposed to walk off, to disappear, you've got to let him. You've got to let history fix itself."

"Don't you get it, boy? History can't be fixed now. It was broken bad enough the first time through. And all the time-travelin's made it worse."

"What about your time-traveling? You thought coming back here to save Jeremiah would change all that?"

"When that Mr. Howe and I broke in, we both knew I was willing to take the time jump. The idea was to go back far enough to stop the whole Project Split Second, if I could. I didn't know it would land me all the way back here.

"So, when I did find myself this far back, in the living days of the Good Word, I figured maybe I could still give history a push in the right direction. An even bigger push, if I could help save the life of Jeremiah . . . help him stick around longer."

"But you just said history can't be fixed."

"Not the one we already have, boy." He rubs his head. "I'm talkin' about comin' up with a whole new history. A better one."

"Is that what they wanted to do in Project Split Second? What my mom wanted to do?"

It's just one more thing I don't find out about my mom. The Gehenna-woman speaks up again, after Jeremiah has been standing calmly for a few moments, tightly surrounded by some of the crowd, who are still deciding whether to let him go or to kill him.

"Let him pass," the woman says. "Let him gather his seeds. Maybe he can do some good outside Jerusalem's broken walls. He was no particular use inside them." And for a moment, everyone seems calmer, like they all let their breath out at once. Jeremiah grabs a homemade spear from one of the men's hands, then breaks off the tip, turning it into a walking stick. He looks like he's ready to go.

"But leave the goat-demon here," the woman adds, "until we decide what to do with him."

There goes the calmness. Right away, someone in the crowd makes a move. People are getting jostled, and my first thought is that someone is going to hurt Jeremiah after all, because that seems to be what usually happens to prophets, anyway.

Except this guy isn't coming for Jeremiah. Whoever he is, he pushes past him and comes toward us. I can see his white hair over the heads of everyone else. It's someone moving fast—

Toward Thea, who is with Naftali and the Bearded Boy.

Naftali's the one he grabs.

It's not just anyone from the crowd. It's Rolf.

He must've been keeping low, using the crowd as cover, until he was close to us. And I finally get a real good look at him, now that he's all grown up.

That was his white hair. But now his skin stretches over his face in a weird way, and his eyes look like they're getting ready to pop out of his face. But he's still just a Dragon Jerk kid, as far as I'm concerned.

And of course, being Rolf, he's holding a gun.

Now he turns his attention to me. "Giff me your hat, so I can get out of here," he says with just a trace of his old accent. "Before I haff to hurt one of these kids."

"You promised you wouldn't let them hurt me," Naftali says, almost crying, looking at me.

Right. I did. No more soldiers, no more being scared.

I don't want that to be a lie. It's too easy for grownups to lie to kids, and I don't want to become that kind of grownup.

And maybe I'm more like A.J. than I realized, because as I look into Naftali's scared eyes, I realize I do want to try to make history turn out better.

His, anyway.

"Are you listening!?" Rolf barks at me.

I am. If I'm going to help Naftali, I don't have a choice.

Chapter Seventeen

Thea: Strangers

My friend Eli will do whatever he can to help Naftali, but I don't think he should give away the soft helmet—the "cap" that allows him to journey through time. Rolf Royd wants it, in exchange for the boy's life.

I believe instead we need to devise another plan.

I'm not sure what that plan should be. Huldah might know. But she stays down below, tending to the sick. She refuses to come up because she is afraid, I believe, that she couldn't survive the heartbreak of what has happened to her city.

Eli was forced to decide whether to give away his "cap" after Rolf, the time traveler from the Third Reich, snuck up on us. Our attention was elsewhere. Mine was with the two boys, Naftali and James. They've both been cast aside by history, or, perhaps, swept away by it, the way Eli and I have been. Each has losses, their entire families taken: In Naftali's case, they appear to have been hauled away to slavery by the invading soldiers. In the case of James—who calls himself the Bearded Boy by way of making something of an entertainment of himself—he was told by authorities that his parents vanished in a mysterious incident—similar, perhaps, to the way Eli lost his own mother. Eli and I, meanwhile, have become victims of another mob, survivors in Yerushalayim who are deciding whether to kill us.

The people here have survived a calamity even worse than the fires in Alexandria. They've seen family members killed by an invading army or taken into slavery. And though like the mobs ruled by Brother Tiberius in Alexandria, the people here are motivated by fear, they are also motivated by their broken hearts. They want nothing else to cause them hurt, and the arrivals, first of me and Eli and then of K'lion and the group he calls his "carnival," only terrified them more.

They seem to think that getting rid of us, and of Jeremiah—who, I gather, routinely chastised them to listen to their god, and perhaps even blamed them for their troubles—might protect them from this heartbreak.

They are wrong, of course.

As I am discovering, nothing can really protect you from that.

So the survivors here were deciding whether to harm us in order to prevent more harm to themselves. If Eli kept his cap, we could disappear if we had to, but how many could we take with us? And what would happen to the others we might have to leave behind? Especially to those younger than us, like James, the Bearded Boy?

I had been translating for him and Naftali, so

they could converse—could keep themselves calm while our fates were being decided.

"So are you an Essene?" Naftali asked James.

"I don't know what that is," James replied.

"They're priests," Naftali explained. "Holy men. With no haircut."

I made a cutting motion with my fingers around my hair as I translated the words for James.

"Living in the desert," Naftali added.

"I'm no priest," James said. "That's for sure. I done some mean things before Rocket took me in. I used to steal food when I had to."

"At least you had food around to steal," Naftali said.

I was trying to keep them talking to each other, but wished I could serve them breakfast instead.

I was getting hungry myself.

That's when Rolf struck, just as he did back in the caves with Merlin and Arthur, only this time he didn't have to use a sword—he had a gun. I have come to know guns in my travels.

He grabbed Naftali and demanded Eli's cap. Then he threatened Naftali.

And now during all these slow, stretched-out moments while Eli is deciding what to do, Rolf's cold gaze reaches me as well. "You, too? Will I never be rid of any of you?"

For a moment, it appears he might try using the weapon on me. I already know what his Reich was capable of. I remember flying over the field, in K'lion's time-ship, watching the mother and child as the German soldier—the good soldier—took aim at both of them.

I remember the clap of thunder then.

And I am not going to let that happen now.

You won't.

The voice again. It is coming back, in occasional wisps, though I had hoped never to hear it again at all, now that the slow pox has passed through me. I have enough to think about.

"I want your hat, Danger Boy," Rolf spits at Eli again. "Or I will start shooting."

"How do you know about Danger Boy?" Eli asks.

"Do you think that just because the stupid Americans made a show of kicking me out of their secret program, I am no longer informed? That because of a mere thing like public appearances, I stopped working on my own? Or that I don't still have allies on the inside?"

"What do you mean, 'public appearances'?" Eli asks him.

It is the one called Andrew Jackson who answers: "They had to pretend to fire Rolf from Project Split Second when a newspaper ran a story about what he'd done as a Nazi."

"We haff since taken care of the newspapers," Rolf answers. "They were too stupid to see *I* was the only one with the nerve to do what needed to be done with Project Split Second. None of the others had it. Not even your mother." He grins.

"What about my mother?" Eli steps toward him. The people around us are getting nervous again, more nervous than they already were.

"*Please,*" Naftali says, whimpering. And I find that my own fear is slowly being replaced by anger. Anger at bullies who think history belongs only to them.

"Let's talk about your hat," Rolf says to Eli. "If I had known about your Danger Boy project sooner, perhaps I could have prevented your stupidly crossing my path in San Francisco during the war, then crossing it again in England."

"Let him go, if it's me you want," Eli tells him.

In reply, Rolf fires his gun in the air.

Naftali screams, then jerks against Rolf's arms, but Rolf holds on to him. "Babylonian," Naftali whispers to me.

I try to keep Naftali's eyes trained on mine, so he can keep his own terror at bay.

Eli is still uncertain what to do.

"Your hat," Rolf repeats. "I could care less about you. It is your hat I want. We shall end your stupid blundering through time right now."

Tears roll from Naftali's eyes, then he shuts them hard, hoping, I think, to make all this go away. "You promised," he squeaks out in another whisper.

My friend Eli unclips his soft helmet from his belt and holds it in his hands. "Don't hurt him," he says. "Don't hurt any of them because of me."

"Just give me that, so I can leave this landscape of broken Jews."

Rolf is speaking English. Only a few of us understand what is going on.

"Release the boy." Someone else understands the situation, though: Jeremiah.

I have not been out of my pox dream state long, but I believe that, like Huldah, he is regarded as something of a prophet. Perhaps he is looked upon as Mother was in Alexandria—someone who says things out loud that make others uncomfortable.

"Be quiet!" a woman in the crowd shouts. "You have nothing more to say in Jerusalem! We told you to go plant your seeds!"

"Even your own people are against you. Out of the way, old fool," Rolf says in the Hebrew tongue. Jeremiah's eyes widen. "Oh yes," Rolf adds. "We learned the language of the dead. For academic reasons. A few permitted traces of your race, which we were going to eliminate."

"Even the Babylonians didn't succeed in that," Jeremiah says. "We are not dead yet."

Rolf appears surprised by this response. Perhaps he was expecting something more fearful.

"You are a ridiculous old man," Rolf says at last. "You should have left when you had the chance." And with that, he moves to strike Jeremiah in the head with his gun.

But Jeremiah swings back with his walking staff.

"No!" Naftali bites Rolf's arm. And before I can reach Naftali and pull him away, Rolf strikes him in the head with the gun. I see a trickle of blood in his hair.

"Stop that, you bully!" James reaches Rolf ahead of me and kicks him in the legs. Rolf is about to swing back and hit him when Eli charges Rolf and knocks him down.

The gun bounces away.

"He's getting the Babylonian!" Naftali tells me, then looks at the blood on his fingers.

"You'll be all right," I tell him, and pull him close. I tear a piece of my clothing off—I am still wearing the robelike garment I was given when Eli and I were imprisoned by his own government—and begin wrapping it around his head.

The loose gun is picked up by another of the time travelers, the one named Rocket.

"Shoot him!" Rolf yells. "Shoot all of them!"

Rocket looks at Rolf and Eli struggling on the ground, then puts the gun in his pocket.

"What are you doing!?" Rolf screams. "You saw what they did to me!"

"I saw," Rocket said. "It's what I always wanted to do to you every time you beat me!"

Rolf's eyes narrow. "You wouldn't dare—" He can't finish, because Eli tries to pin him to the dirt.

Rocket watches his grandfather fight with my friend. The people of Yerushalayim watch, too, still from a distance, willing to let all of us hurt each other.

Rocket paces over to Rolf, yelling at him, but does nothing to help Eli. "I did everything you asked! Did *more* than you asked—took care of the genetic experiments from all your secret programs for you and rounded them up whenever they escaped!" he says, pointing at K'lion.

"'Genetic experiment?'" K'lion repeats. "No, I am merely a wandering *tkkkt!* Saurian."

For the trouble of speaking up, K'lion elicits more cries of "Goat-demon!"

But Rocket isn't finished with his grandfather yet. "And did you ever thank me? I took all your failed lab projects with me into the streets and kept your Odd-Lots Carnival, your freak show, out of sight, so nobody would ask too many questions."

"I am not some freak-show experiment!" the Bearded Boy says, pointing at K'lion.

"Neither *pttt!* am I!" K'lion repeats. "I am an outlaw!"

Eli now has Rolf pinned under him.

"There was a time," Rolf hisses at Rocket, "when you wouldn't be allowed to do this to me."

"We aren't in that time anymore," Rocket says to him.

"No matter what time we're in"—and even with all the dirt on Rolf's face, I can see that he's wearing a grin—"little Danger Boy here will be interested to know I was the last person to see his mother alive."

"What!?" It's just enough to distract Eli, and Rolf flips him over and now has my friend pinned under him.

"Not bad for an old man, eh?" Rolf yells. "The *Drachenjungen* never grow old and never forget!"

"Stop it, Grandfather! Stop it now." Rocket has taken the gun back out of his pocket and aims it at Rolf's head. "Let him go. It's my turn to be pointing the gun now."

"You wouldn't dare," Rolf tells him, "no matter what time we're in."

It is unclear whether Rocket will actually fire the gun, but K'lion has seen enough and leaps over, knocking Rocket down to the ground. "No! No more mammals dancing with guns!"

And then, with his tail, he knocks Rolf off of Eli.

I consider these both good and fine actions, but the people around us do not. K'lion's sudden movement and yelling—the actions of a "goat-demon"—cause everything that has been pent up to come exploding out in a fury.

They rush toward us; they even jump on one another, everyone hitting and throwing things.

"You cry for peace!" Jeremiah yells. "But there is no peace! Stop this! Stop!"

But no one is listening to him. They are too busy fighting. Someone has K'lion's tail, and Eli and Rocket crouch with their backs to each other to keep from being overwhelmed.

I grab Naftali and James and try to move them out of harm's way.

K'lion now hops around, getting pelted with even more rocks. A.J. tries to protect him, and I pull Naftali and James under an overhang.

But in the confusion, Rolf has crawled over to where Eli's soft helmet landed earlier and now clutches it in his hand.

"No!" Eli yells.

Rolf puts it on his head, and nothing happens.

Eli sees what's going on and tries to get over to Rolf, but the crowd blocks his way.

"Let me through!"

"Let him pass!" I yell in Hebrew, but no one is listening to anyone.

Rolf takes the cap on and off, but still nothing happens. There is an artificial covering on it, which Eli calls Thickskin, that prevents immediate contact with the material.

Rolf must know this, too, as he starts scratching at the covering.

Naftali and James hold on to me.

"Gehenna-marked!" It is the woman who has been accusing us all along, and now she grabs at me from above, reaching into the overhang, pulling me away from the boys.

"I knew it!" she screams. "Bringing us nothing but misery!"

Eli has fought his way to within arm's reach of Rolf, who puts the cap back on his head one more time . . .

. . . and vanishes.

And with him, perhaps, our only chance of getting back to Eli's time.

Eli groans and slumps to his knees. I think he's hurt, but Rolf's seeming display of magic increases the crowd's rage against us to a lethal level. Naftali and James are both crying, terrified, and before I can even move to help anyone, the woman who is attacking me drops down in front of me, then steps toward me, holding a club in her hand . . .

. . . when something behind me catches her eye, and she stops and points over my shoulder.

"Look," she says to no one in particular. "Look!" she shouts now, pointing, and though I don't think anyone can hear her, other people in the rioting crowd see the same thing she does, and more and more of them stop and point and say, "Look," until finally, you can hear each of their voices again.

"Look. It's her."

"It's her!"

Huldah.

Huldah has come up, out of her cave.

Back up here, to the surface, to the world. To the ruins of her city.

And behind her are several of the slow pox victims, the Gehanna-marked, the people with

Seraphic plague or whatever name it goes by, other survivors, coming up out of the darkness with her.

But I don't know if they'll listen to Huldah, since they haven't been listening to Jeremiah.

"Jeremiah is right," Huldah says. "You will never have what you seek if you keep tearing each other to shreds."

"We don't want any more strangers around us," the Gehenna-woman tells her, still brandishing her club.

I seek out the faces of my friends in the crowd and see K'lion—who, of course, looks the most strangerlike of all—and then Eli. And then I look at Eli's shirt.

There is English on it, which I am surprised I can read. I am growing increasingly familiar with his native tongue.

All of which gives me an idea.

Chapter Eighteen

Eli: Gimel, Gimel

583 B.C.E.

It was my jersey that finally calmed everyone down and kept them from throwing rocks at us or doing something worse.

My jersey, that is, and the way Andrew Jackson Williams celebrates the Jewish New Year.

First, it was Thea's idea to translate and let everyone know what my shirt said: House of David. Though in Hebrew it sounded like "B'eight Dah-veed."

"House of David. See?" Thea explained. "He's with the House of David, too." A.J. confirmed the translation; no one tried to explain what base-ball was, but the idea that I was with "House of David" could also mean I was related to King David.

We didn't bother to correct anyone.

Of course, that made some of them madder — they thought I was claiming to be some kind of anointed or chosen one who was supposed to be descended from David himself.

So it still might not have worked, except that Huldah came over to have a closer look herself. She couldn't read English, but she looked at the garment, ran her fingers over it, and noticed the two mysterious letters sewn on the inside.

"*Gimel! Gimel!*" she said, reading them. So they *were* Hebrew.

"He has two gimels on this garment." Huldah turned and explained to the survivors. She un-buttoned my shirt enough so she could lift the flap and point out the letters to everyone else. It was a little embarrassing. "The two gimels refer to reward and punishment — the sign of conse-quence for every action."

"What?" I whispered to Thea.

"In Hebrew, each letter equals a number. *Gimel* equals the number three," she whispered back, speaking fast. "And each letter, each number, has special cosmic meaning. The gimel refers to balance and to choice—each choice bringing its own outcome, for good or bad."

"Like history itself?"

"Yes. Like everything. In balance between light and dark. Mother would sometimes study the hidden meanings of holy texts, including Hebrew letters, in the library, especially with visiting scholars who were always trying to unlock ancient mysteries."

"What hidden meanings?" I asked.

"It is what your father does with his science. Tries to make more sense of things."

"So then, this is like the Hebrew version of my uniform number? Number thirty-three? It's part of the replica? Or does that mean it's a real jersey?"

"You are asking me a baseball question?" Thea wondered.

"I guess not."

So gimel gimel was Green Bassett's uniform number: two threes next to each other, for number 33. And each three had special significance in Hebrew. Someone in the House of David must have known that. Did they know it just might have saved the lives of me and my friends?

There really is a lot of stuff going on in the world that we can't see.

"The stranger's garment," Huldah was saying, "reminds us of what Jeremiah told us, when he said, 'O, House of David, bring justice in the morning.' He also asked for deliverance from the oppressor for those who have been robbed or scorned, for us to escape the consequence of someone else's thoughtless, cruel actions, and to make choices that are wise and that allow us to walk in God's way.

"It is morning," she said, gesturing to the sun and the remaining traces of melting frost, "and everyone in this place, even these strangers, are part of the House of David now." She lifted her hand, sweeping past the wreckage-strewn horizon.

"And this is that house. This ruined place. It is up to us to decide what kind of house — what kind of home — will rise up this time."

"She's good," A.J. whispered to me. "A long time ago, I was against women preachers. But she's good. If I still had my pulpit in Vinita, I'd invite her to speak some gospel.

"Well, no sense havin' ears if you're not gonna listen to what's bein' said. I'm gonna finish my rebuildin' project."

He walked over to where we'd started to build an altar earlier. Some of the stones had been knocked over again. He picked one up and set it on top of another.

Huldah saw him, and then she lifted up a smaller rock and put it on top of where there had once been a wall.

The Gehenna-woman picked up a rock. For just a second, I thought she might throw it at one of us. "There's nothing left to lose by trying," she said. Then she laid it on the remains of the wall, next to Huldah's.

After that, everyone else started to pick up rocks and stones and pieces of rubble, too.

By the time we stopped, it was late afternoon and everyone had worked up a sweat, even in the cool winter air.

It looked like a section of one of the temple's walls was halfway standing again, in a kind of lopsided way. And leading from that was a lined pathway up to the altar that A.J. had finished.

Now A.J. wants to put that altar to use. "I guess it'd only be right to make an offerin', since it's the New Year and all." A.J. looks around, then takes something out of his pocket. It's a little scrap of cloth, I guess, but it's old and muddy. All I can see is the word REACH on it.

He lays it on the altar.

"What's that?" I ask.

"Piece of an old baseball. Made by the A. J. Reach Company. They're out of business now."

"Why are you leaving it here?"

"That baseball, son, is the reason I'm back here, in Jerusalem. With you. It's what got me started on this whole time-travel business. Since I'm not sure if any of us are gettin' back now, especially since your cap is gone and all, well, I thought I'd try to make my peace with things."

Neither of us says anything for a moment.

"There's a lot you haven't told me, isn't there?"

"Well, for starters, that's all that's left of a baseball once used by Satchel Paige."

"That's not what I meant."

"Well, it all starts with Green Bassett."

"That's not what I meant, either."

"Actually, son, it kind of is." He looks around—people are quiet now, at least in the sense they've stopped actively trying to kill us or drive us away. "Let's take a walk and try to find Jeremiah."

"If he's gone, we shouldn't try to bring him back. That's not how history is supposed to play out."

"I just want to say goodbye, son."

I look around to see if Naftali or James want to come with us, but they're gone. "I think she took 'em back down to the cave," A.J. says, watching me turning my head. "The boys. I think Thea went back down there to wash 'em up, get 'em away from all the riotin' folks up here."

"I should see her."

"You should. But you should find out some things first."

We walk down the stone path, past the newly rebuilt wall, out toward the fields. We pass the remains of what Naftali told me used to be the palace. A.J. points to it.

"That's where the kings lived. They're all gone now. The very last one had to watch his own children die. After that, they blinded him."

"Jeez. That's horrendous." I think of Thea, who had to go through something like that, but in reverse. "History is really awful."

"Lotta scary things in the Bible, son, I won't kid you. It can be a fearsome book. Did Huldah ever tell you about the king she worked for?"

"No."

"Name of Josiah. He was a bit earlier. Called on her to interpret one of the Bible scrolls they'd found stashed away in the temple. Make sense of the word of God, as it were."

"Did she?"

"As much as anyone can. They added a lot of new laws to the books after that, trying to keep people on the straight and narrow. But laws only work for a while, if people don't feel things"— and now it's his turn to tap his chest— "in here."

"Why are people tapping their hearts so much?"

"I guess we're all havin' lots of strong feelings back here in the Holy Land."

"Is that why you became a preacher, 'cause you believe everything happened just like it says in the Bible? What about all the things it doesn't explain? Like where my mom is or whether we're ever going to get back? Are we stuck here for- ever? What about that?"

A.J. picks up a stick from the ground—a long piece of wood, not a tree branch, but a piece of what used to be a wall or a pillar. "I became a preacher 'cause I think there's something bigger than all of us out there, a Great Mystery that we all need to tend to."

"Well, I have plenty of mysteries."

A.J. takes a rock and throws it in the air, then swings the stick at it. He gives it a pretty good hit, and it skitters into the desert.

"Your mother, son. She disappeared in the late 1960s."

I wish I wasn't so used to my stomach falling all the time. "So is my mom still around, still in this world, or not?

"She'd come out to Vinita to see me."

"She still knew you?"

"She stayed with Project Split Second after the war. All through the '50s and '60s. The whole cold war. She never wanted time travel to be used as a weapon."

He throws another rock and hits it.

"She was with the project all the way through, trying to make sure it never got out of hand, was never used to hurt people."

"Well, how far did they get?"

"They got as far as sending a couple of test subjects through time."

"Really?" That doesn't necessarily sound like she kept it from hurting anyone. "Who?"

"Me, for starters. And Rolf."

Now it's so weird, I have to sit down. A.J. keeps taking batting practice, stopping for a moment to stare at the wood in his hand. "This thing I'm usin' for a bat actually came from a palace, son. A palace the kings probably thought would last forever. Nothin' lasts forever."

Not even Project Split Second, apparently. He tells me that Rolf was put in charge of the program after the war, because, as part of the *Drachenjungen*, he was supposed to know a lot about time travel. It didn't matter how he got the knowledge.

"It was that Operation Paperclip stuff again," A.J. says. "Puttin' Nazis all over our own government."

But my mom stayed on as one of the research scientists. She was the one always saying they weren't ready to test on humans yet. "But ol'

Rolfie always wondered what the point was if you *didn't* test it on humans. What was it gonna be used for, anyway? So he started to look for volunteers.

"And finally, he had one. Me." A.J. swings the wood and hits another single.

"Why you?"

"It got me out of an Army hospital, where I'd been for a few years." *Whack!* A foul tip.

"Why were you there?"

"It was the kind of place they keep people who claim to have 'seen things.' People who might cause a certain kind of trouble."

Apparently, a lot of the trouble started after I'd jumped into the dimensional rift at Fort Point, where my mom was. A.J. tried to jump in after me. "I didn't think you should go alone, son. It didn't seem right."

But my mom held on to him by his heels and pulled him back out. He'd been halfway in the time stream. In spacetime.

"Halfway in?" I ask. "What was that like?"

A.J. shakes his head. "It just confirmed the

mysteries. But they kept me in Army hospitals for years after that, for 'observation,' as they called it. Occasionally, Rolf would come and ask me what I knew."

And apparently, just when Rolf was ready to get A.J. his release, to do a "volunteer jump" through time, a small paper, the *National Weekly Truth*, published a story about Rolf's background as a Nazi.

"Some kind of tabloid or something," A.J. says. *Whack!* "But then the regular papers picked it up, and our government was so embarrassed, they had to let Rolf go."

"So what happened then?"

"He tried to steal some WOMPERs and do his own experiments, his own time travel. Your mom thought that might be a good time to shut down the program. She leaked some more details to the press, some people in Congress were gettin' upset . . ." *Whack!* "And she arranged to get my release from the hospital. I had to sign all these forms, swearin' never to tell what I'd seen."

"But you did."

"In my book. *The Time Problem.* Published by the same folks that publish that *Truth* paper. But I thought people had the right to know. Your mom thought I was in danger. So she came out to Oklahoma to see me. I'd gone home by then, to get out of government service and start preachin'. But that didn't pay well, and I had to find a way to support it. So I opened a motel."

Whack!

"Turns out somebody else followed your mom out there, too."

My stomach can't really fall any farther. "Rolf."

"Your mother was bringin' somethin' she wanted me to have, for safekeeping."

"What was that?"

"One of the last-known captured WOMPER particles. Which the Split Second folks needed, to trigger a time reaction." *Whack!*

Even though Rolf was officially out of Project Split Second by then, he was still doing work for the government. "Unauthorized" experiments that were actually, according to A.J., completely authorized. By somebody with power.

But something went wrong when Rolf followed my mom. "Maybe there was a fight and the WOMPER got loose, but whatever it was, it triggered a time reaction right there in Vinita. I was runnin' my motel at the time and didn't quite realize what had happened till later. Till right after a couple of guests in particular checked into my place, who didn't even seem to know what time they were in."

"Me and my dad? On that trip we were taking cross-country?"

Whack!

"Yeah."

"And my mom was there, in Vinita? When we were? When we were so close?"

"Turns out she'd disappeared, along with Rolf, in another time reaction. They must've been closest to whatever it was that happened, because they pretty much vanished for a while. Well, not Rolf. He popped up again in the early 2000s but had to keep a low profile till he could get his hands on another WOMPER."

"So my mom is gone again?"

"Last I knew, she was in the '60s for a while. Maybe you can catch her back there."

"And what about you?"

Whack! A.J. could've maybe gone into base-ball to support his preaching. But then again, with so much going on, how can you concentrate on baseball? The House of David guys must have always known where their families were, in order to do it.

"As for me, son, I guess I had a little accident of my own after that. The government guys, DARPA and some of the other agencies, tried to put me back in the hospital after your mom disappeared, so I wouldn't talk about what I knew. But I still had something they hadn't counted on."

"What was that?"

"A baseball."

"The one you left on the altar?"

"Yup."

"The one from Satchel Paige?"

"And Green Bassett. Yup." *Whoosh!*

For the first time, he misses. The rock falls straight down into the sand.

"When did you meet him?"

"When he came to Vinita for some exhibition games." *Whack!* A.J. hits the next one, and it flies over some nearby rocks, disappearing from view.

Someone says, *"OW!"*

A.J. and I look at each other, then scramble over to see who it is.

It's Jeremiah, in the late-afternoon sun. He stands up when he sees us, rubbing his head. "Someone's always throwing stones at me."

"It was an accident," A.J. tells him. In Hebrew. "We didn't know anyone else was here."

"I came out to start planting, like I said I would." There's a cloth bag near Jeremiah's feet, full of seeds. "I found these in the wreckage of the granary, in the midst of all that confusion. Hopefully, there'll be enough wheat and barley and beans by next spring."

"We have to make it through winter first," A.J. tells him.

"Did you try rebuilding the temple again?" Jeremiah asks.

"A little," A.J. replies. "Everybody needs something to look forward to."

"God doesn't really worry about our buildings," Jeremiah says. "That isn't where my people need to rebuild."

I expect him to start tapping his chest again, but he just looks at A.J.

"I know. But sometimes, you gotta take people there one step at a time."

Jeremiah looks away from us, out over the horizon.

"I expect you're takin' a few steps of your own," A.J. continues. "You're still plannin' on leavin'." He doesn't ask it as a question.

"After I finish planting, yes. Jerusalem is better off without me now. I bring up too many old memories, of pasts that can't be changed."

"But—" I start in English. A.J. shakes his head at me. I guess he's right. Even if I could tell Jeremiah that maybe the past can be changed all kinds of ways after all, that might not make him feel any better. He might even want to start time-traveling!

And we don't need another one of those.

"I believe I will head toward Egypt," he says. A.J. nods. "Perhaps no one will know me there. And what about you?"

A.J. looks at me. "I think we're stuck with Jerusalem for a while, and Jerusalem's stuck with us."

I've been trying not to think about this. But with my cap gone, and no one here with WOM-PERs or a lab full of experiments, I realize he's right.

I'll be spending the rest of my life here. With Thea. And A.J. And all those people Clyne brought. I won't ever see my parents again.

I'll grow up here. And then what?

Marry Thea?

That's too weird to even think about.

And I sure won't ever get to play Barnstorm-ers again.

"A good time to meet!" Clyne bounds over, apparently having hopped across the sands after us.

Jeremiah takes a few steps back, crouching a

little, still not sure what to make of Clyne. He stands straight after a few moments but keeps his distance. "And I believe it will be good if I am no longer seen in the company of a goat-demon."

"I have been searching you out, friends!" Clyne says to us. "I believe I may have a way *znnnkt!* to get us home."

Chapter Nineteen

Eli: Slaversaur

Any day now, we should know if this works. So far, it's been three.

Clyne's idea was to open up a dimensional rift. He said he got the idea when he saw the scrap of the Reach baseball reflecting the rays of the setting sun "in multi-*tizzyng* many-vectored ways. As if the shred of cloth contained some plasmechanical material."

"Well," A.J. said, "that's because I reckon it does."

The whole thing began when he'd actually met Green Bassett, right before he disappeared.

It was in Vinita, after an exhibition game against one of Satchel Paige's traveling all-star squads from the Negro Leagues.

"I saw Bassett the mornin' after the first game, walkin' out of town, kinda like he was in disguise, a big overcoat on him, even on a sticky Oklahoma day, with a hat pulled low over his eyes, carryin' somethin' in the kinda case you might put a fishin' pole in, or a shotgun. Though once you figured out you were lookin' at a ballplayer, you could guess it was a baseball bat. I was on a store porch, with an Orange Crush on my lips, when I saw him. 'Hey, Green Bassett!' I yelled.

"He put a finger to his mouth, like I'd already spilled the beans. 'Where you goin'?' I asked, 'cause I knew he was s'posed to have another game against Satchel Paige that night."

"Paige could pitch two days in a row?" I interrupted.

"If he had to, son. Had to make hay any way he could, since they weren't lettin' black men into the majors back then. 'I need to go away awhile,' he told me, ' 'cause things ain't exactly like I thought.'

" 'What things?' I asked him.

"That's when he flipped me the Reach ball. 'Ask Paige how he learned to throw spitters like this one,' he said. 'I never struck out on three straight pitches before. Never. I'm going to New Orleans to see for myself.' And then he left town, son. He left baseball, too. No one ever saw him after that."

"Did you ever find out what he meant?"

"I snuck into the ballpark the next day. Ol' Satchel wouldn't tell me, but he showed me after the game. Everyone else had left the park. A spitter, son, like you've never seen before. Took a little resin bag he had, only there wasn't no resin in it. 'My special sauce,' Paige said. And he dabbed a little on the ball, looked around, then threw a pitch that gave off sparks and zigged and zagged, and almost seemed to stop before it reached the plate. Like a ball out of a cartoon.

" 'Learned that down in Louisiana,' Paige told me. 'Only use it when I have to. Against batters like Green Bassett. Still, I may have to give that pitch up. It unnerves even me.'

"I knew what he meant. The whole thing seemed unnatural, even for a pitcher as great as ol' Satchel. Well, son, in those days, I was young myself, and thought about ballplayin'."

So he *did* have other options besides the motel.

"That was before preachin' took ahold of me. So I headed off to New Orleans, armed with only the vague descriptions Paige had given me of where he had gone to get that 'special sauce' that made the ball fly around so crazy. I wanted to learn its secret. And I got as far as a tree."

I knew exactly which tree he meant. The one in the bayou outside of old New Orleans, the city that used to be there before all the hurricanes struck. The place I'd visited with Thea and Clyne. The spot where the Saurian time-ship had crashed in the early 1800s, outside Lake Ponchartrain. It created a place—I guess Clyne would call it a nexus—where escaped slaves could just . . . "disappear."

"The special sauce? . . ." I asked, beginning to put the pieces together. "From the crash site? It was still there?"

"Material from the alien ship, piloted by your goat-demon friend. I know that now."

"Plasmechanics!" Clyne chirped. "Even a small amount on a *snkkt!* base-sphere could change its quantum position in spacetime! Just a *znggt!* fraction! Enough to make the orb seem *gerk-skizzy!* as if it wasn't quite solid when it moved through air!"

In other words, when a pitch usually leaves a pitcher's hand, the ball goes forward in space and time, arriving at the plate or against the bat. But if it had plasmechanical material on it, like Paige's, it wouldn't move straight through time in the normal way. It'd be off by a microsecond here or there, just enough to make it a lot harder to hit. Maybe impossible.

"Your friend's small reminder prompted me to search out *sknggg!* my own pockets, where, in another moment of *merrikus,* I discovered I had plasmechanical material, too, residue from the explosions and hot weapon beams blasting *knnng!* my way while in mammalian custody! Enough here to open a dimensional rift that we might time-journey through!"

"How would we do that?" I wanted to get all the details before I started to feel at all hopeful.

Clyne reached into his fairly worn-out Saurian jump suit and pulled out a handful—clawful—of . . . goo.

Plasmechanical goo.

"Secret sauce," A.J. said.

The goo almost seemed to be humming.

"This was from my time-ship. A beam weapon superheated a section of it in your *pnnng!* tunnel jail and created a small *tnnng!* reaction, which allowed me to escape from the room. Perhaps if we superheated *pkkt!* this, we could create a similar *boom*-like moment of rift-shifting."

I was like one of the people Huldah was talking about—afraid to get too hopeful, because I knew how easily things could go wrong. But then again, weren't she and A.J. and Jeremiah saying you still had to have *some* hope, no matter what? Just to go on?

"Well, Clyne, we have a problem: we don't *have* any way to superheat it. We still have to wait around a couple thousand years for beam weapons to be invented. We can't just throw fastballs. Even Satchel Paige fastballs. Sparks aren't enough."

"Fire?" The word was spoken behind me, in English. Thea.

She'd come back with Naftali and James. They were all scrubbed up, and she'd even managed to get James's hair wet and comb it back, so that he looked kind of like a kid who was wearing a Bigfoot costume for Halloween, except he'd also been invited to a girl's tea party, so he had to try to look neat.

There was even a fresh bandage on Naftali's head.

"Fire," Thea repeated, gesturing to the small fires that were all around us. After even just one day of building, the place seemed more like a camp, a settlement of some sort, instead of just a ruin.

There were walls, pieces of structures, for

people to huddle behind. There were several groups around the different campfires, and each seemed to be sharing what it had—from bits of food to scraps of blanket. Some people had huddled together to doze off.

I didn't know if that was enough to make a city, or a community, but at least it wasn't a war.

Clyne shook his head. "Fire remains not heat-ful enough," he told Thea. "But if we are trapped here muchly"—and then he broke into one of his overly toothy smiles—"perhaps I can work on a way to *plkkkt!* harness solar rays"—he pointed to the moon—"in some kind of focused energy *bttt!* burst."

"You mean sunshine?" A.J. asked.

"Yes."

"When the sun's up there, instead of the moon?"

"*Snkkkt!* Yes."

"Reflected off somethin' like a mirror?"

"*Kngaa!*"

We all waited for Clyne to finish his sentence.

"That is the Saurian word for *yes*."

A.J. nodded and looked at me. "Well, boy? How 'bout it? I mighta had the Reach in my pocket, but the goat-demon has the sauce! I got one more thing, too. But this one's meant for you." And A.J. reached into his shirt and took out the small wrapped mirror I'd seen earlier.

You are reflected in your friends, family, and times!

One man's family. Mine. And some of those who had become my family were there with me: Thea and Clyne. Maybe even A.J., as a kind of crazy grandpa who doesn't always appear to make much sense, except when you listen real close.

"Well, how long would it take using this?" I asked, unwrapping the mirror. Some of the camp-fires glinted in its reflection.

"Tomorrow we begin our field observations to find out! *Stnnkt!*"

"What if it doesn't work, K'lion?" Thea asked.

"Then we have plenty of time to consider the next *znnnng!* field experiment."

I don't know if Clyne was attempting a joke for our benefit or stating what he considered a scientific fact. Thea just nodded without saying anything, then turned her attention to finding some food for the boys.

Later that night, we made a fire of our own near the wall by the path that led to A.J.'s altar. It kept some of the wind away, and we all huddled together and even got a little sleep.

I'm pretty sure I wasn't the only one who dreamed of home.

And so, here we've been for three days. Clyne has worked with A.J. to keep positioning the mirror so the plasmechanical material directly receives the beam.

"Your body vibrates in *sknng!* time-moving resonance," Clyne explained. "Once the plasme-chanics reach a certain heatitude, they will explode small but distinctly, like that starchy snack food consumed during visual entertainments."

"Popcorn?"

"Yes! *Klllkt!* Like popcorn. Creating a small but exploitable rift in space-*tnngg!*-time. A big version of the ball-base *stkkt!* sparks you saw."

"But then how do we *use* it, Clyne?" I asked him. "There's no ship. No atom-altering cap to put on."

"I believe you should stick your hand through the *vnnng!* vortex when the rift occurs."

"What about the rest of me?"

"In theory, you will be pulled along, since the reverse particle charge particular to you should then course through your whole body."

"And what about everybody else?" I asked. "I brought Thea here. I can't leave her. And then all those people who came with you . . ."

"In theory, *we* will be pulled along if we hold on to you, while hoping *sknntng!* for the best, though it is true that the rift may close again swiftly before everyone could get through."

The definitions of "we" and "everyone" eventually shifted. It was just Clyne, Thea, A.J., and me who were trying the time jump. By yesterday, Rocket had decided to stay.

He'd gone off after Rolf disappeared, thinking he could find his grandfather somewhere in the desert and maybe hold him accountable for the things he'd done.

He couldn't. Rolf was gone.

So he'd taken up with the rebuilding idea started by A.J., and helped stacking rocks, moving old burnt timbers, and digging. He'd also go with Naftali and James to take water out to the ground where Jeremiah had planted his seeds.

"It will be good to stay in one place long enough to see something grow from the ground up," he said. "And I like a world where everything is right in front of you." I guess he was tired of living with all of Rolf's secrets and he thought this would be a simpler time.

I still wasn't sure it'd be a good idea for him to stay behind with James, but by Clyne's calculations, only three or four of us, at most, could get back.

So Rocket volunteered to stay, and he'll get his chance to find some kind of happiness a few thousand years before he is born. And maybe some kind of better history will come out of it after all. I guess you can't really put genies back in bottles once they're out, and the time-travel genie has been loose for a while.

"Besides, this might be a good place for a show," Rocket said. "We could cheer people up. We could make a real difference. And anyway," he said, lowering his voice, even though no one but us spoke English, "it might help make up for some of the things my grandfather did."

"Was Rolf *really* your grandfather?" I asked.

"He adopted me as a baby when my parents disappeared after volunteering for one of his experiments. They'd both been with the military. But then Rolf disappeared too, and I grew up in a government facility where they kept . . . well, I'm not allowed to talk about it. But I didn't see him again for many years."

It was the middle of a clear desert day. It was bright and blue in the distance, and it seemed like we were standing in the middle of the world, with every direction stretching out to infinity around us. "There's no one here who can hurt you," I told him.

Sometimes people just need to hear that.

He looked around to be sure, then continued. "Well, I grew up there, and then worked there as an adult—because I had noplace else to go. I was always pretty alone. There were creatures in that place . . . that couldn't be explained. The results of genetic experiments, I think, like James. Or maybe visitors . . . like your lizard friend.

"But mostly you had no idea who else was in there with you. Until one day somebody came in a flying saucer and busted somebody out. I heard the noise outside, and in the commotion, I helped some of the people and creatures in there escape. With me.

"We formed a circus. My circus. We kept a low profile, in small out-of-the-way places, makin' our own way through the world, until suddenly, out of the blue, Rolf was back—like he'd just popped back out of the sky or something.

"He was able to have me tracked down. And

blackmailed me. Said he'd send everyone in my circus — even me — back to that zoo-prison we were in if I didn't cooperate."

" 'Cooperate?' "

"I'd go find things he wanted or needed while he pretended to be a retired old man working as a gardener. I guess being scared like that, looking over my shoulder all the time, made me pretty mean." He sighed, like he was trying to let a few years worth of bad air out of his body. "I think by staying here, I won't have to look over my shoulder so much. That's one of the reasons I went into the desert. I *was* looking for my grandfather, in a way. I wanted to make sure he was really gone this time."

I didn't tell him that with my cap in Rolf's possession, no one can really be sure where Rolf might pop up next or what he might try to do.

"Hey, when you get back," Rocket continued, "will you try to round up Strong Bess and the bat and Silver Eye? I'm not sure if they know what to do out there on their own."

"I'll see what I can do," I said, not really

knowing if I ever *would* get back, or, if I did, whether there was anything at all I could do about finding the missing half of his carnival. It's the way grownups talk to kids half the time, saying "I will" when you can't be sure of anything, pretending the world makes sense when it really doesn't at all.

And as of today, James, the Bearded Boy, said he wanted to stay, too. He and Naftali have found a common bond, like brothers. Orphan brothers, with only each other to rely on.

"It'll be hard for you, James, when Thea goes," I told him. "You won't have her to translate for you."

"But I'll have someone who knows what it's like to be me," he said, talking about Naftali. "And anyway, I'm not even a James."

"You're not?"

"I used to look up profiles of kids on the Comnet, in libraries, sometimes. James Rodney was this kid out in Illinois someplace — about five feet tall, blond hair, blue eyes, played a lot of sports like soccer, golf, even water polo. He had lots of friends. I read about him on the Comsite his family made when they were having some kind of family reunion. I thought: I could be like him. Or maybe, I *wanted* to be like him. To have that same kind of life he had. So I started to call myself James."

Thinking of what Rocket and James had told me, I realized that some of the things A.J. said about Jerusalem were still true. People were still coming here looking for something, hoping, maybe, that they could leave something else behind and walk away feeling better, or luckier, or just less worried.

That's what all of us want, too, even those of us who came here pretty much by accident.

Early this morning, the woman who grabbed at Thea and called her "Gehenna-marked" gave the Bearded Boy a haircut, though all she had to use was a broken piece of sword, scavenged from the temple ruins. Now he just looks like he's going to the tea party, never mind Halloween.

Except, in this case, it's a rock-throwing party with Naftali. It's late afternoon, and they're throwing strikes at the outline of the soldier on the temple wall.

Occasionally, they yell, "Barnstormer!" when they're throwing. I've been able to teach them a couple things about baseball and about having a little fun, no matter what.

"I think things are about to get a little *gerk-skizzy*!" Clyne announces, watching the plas-mechanic goo start to . . . percolate, on the flat white rock where it's been these last three days.

"Hold this, please," A.J. says to Huldah, handing her the mirror. She's come to watch us leave.

"Just to be clear," she says, "the power to perform miracles belongs only to God."

"Well, it'll be a miracle if this really works," I say, thinking that even if we land anywhere—or anytime—near home, we'll still have to figure out where Rolf went and how to get him back and whether we'll need to come back for the other refugees from the Odd-Lots Carnival that we're leaving here in Jerusalem's ruins.

"May God grant you safe passage, wherever you're going now," Huldah says.

"Thank you, Huldah," Thea tells her.

"You're welcome. And perhaps you will find a way to pass along any blessings you may have received here. And take some of this." Huldah hands Thea what looks like a wineskin.

"It's healing water, from the *wadi*. You never know when you might need some."

As the sun begins to set again, a lot of people are standing around their campfires. There are even more fires now; every morning, before setting up the mirror with Clyne, to reflect light on the plasmechanical goo, A.J.'d set up a new cooking fire, to make sure the sparks never went out.

"Always got to give something back," he told me, blowing on some embers.

Over the last couple of days, people have grown to accept us, even if they're not overly fond of us.

And just as it looks like we might have to spend one more night here, Clyne jumps up. "Heating to critical *snggg!* mass!" he says. "We must get in proximate contact with the brewing dimensional *flnnng!* rift!"

The plasmechanical goo has been on top of another small pile of rocks—another altar, really—made by A.J., though this one is a short walk from the temple ruins. The mirror has been propped in another small pile of stones a few feet away, with each of us moving it during the day.

Now, as the sun fades, A.J. takes the mirror and hands it to James, who is part of the crowd that's gathered around us again—though this time, they're here to watch, not to throw rocks.

"Keep this thing aimed right there at all that sauce on those stones," A.J. says, and then he runs over to hold hands with me and Clyne. Well, hold claws with Clyne. Some of the goo is so hot, it pops off the rock, like oil from a skillet, and burns my skin a little. But I don't move.

My other arm is around Thea's waist. She's warm and my fingers fit kinda neatly where her body curves in—which is sort of corny, but I want to keep her close. I can't keep losing everyone.

"Here's hoping we get home," I say.

But where is that, exactly, for each of us? Or even for me?

"Speaking of *snkkkt!* homes," Clyne says, his eyes widening. "I almost forgot! This is for you. I found it in *your* home. The one near Wolf House."

He takes a crumpled envelope out of one of the chrono-suit pockets on his back leg and hands it to me. It has my name on it: ELI. It's an old-fashioned letter, like from when they used to write Comnet messages on paper. But I don't have time to open it.

I stuff it into one of my pockets and put my arm back around Thea as quickly as I can.

There is a loud hum, then a roar and a rush of color and motion like a hard wind has sucked me in. But I know the name of this storm.

We're in the Fifth Dimension.

And then, just as suddenly, we're not.

Chapter Twenty

Eli: Moonglow

2020 C.E.

Dear Eli—

Weird, huh? This is how our grandparents would get in touch with their friends, writing on a piece of paper like this, and waiting forever for the message to get through. I never thought I'd have to do it with you. But all my Comnet messages to you keep bouncing back.

What have you been doing since you moved away? . . .

How do you explain time travel to somebody who hasn't done it? Or wouldn't believe it. Even an old friend who was practically like your brother.

Andy and I grew up together in New Jersey. Discovered Barnstormers together. And I haven't seen him since I moved west with my dad.

His family was on a trip to California when he left this message here. In spite of all the quarantines, they were able to get passes to move around. Probably because his mom is a doctor.

I had a hard time getting a message to you, but I knew we were coming to California, and I thought it'd be cool to see you . . .

But by the time he got here, I was gone—probably several centuries away. My dad wasn't here, either. The Moonglow was abandoned.

It's not abandoned anymore.

Thea and I have been living here since we returned, along with Dad. The government had to shut down the labs in the BART tunnels, after all the accidents there, especially the ones caused by Mr. Howe and A.J. So Dad has been able to come back to the Moonglow to do his experiments, in his own way, on his own terms.

It's a little bit hard getting used to being around him again, after being on my own, kinda, for, well, for thousands of years, in a way.

But he tries to really listen to me now, and I'm getting used to listening to him again. DARPA has to listen to Dad now, too, because things are still going wrong all over.

One of those things is that Clyne and A.J. are lost. The brief dimensional rift Clyne talked about separated us in the Fifth Dimension.

Maybe Clyne's Saurian body reacts differently to direct time travel; he might really need his ship to keep him from landing weeks and miles from where he intended to be. Or maybe he had some leftover plasmechanical goo in his pocket that affected his calculations. And who knows? Maybe A.J. still had part of his lucky Reach baseball in his clothes, too. In any case, neither of them was with Thea and me when we landed.

After we rest up, I expect I'll have to go looking for them.

There seems to be plenty to do. Time is still spinning out of control. A lot of the Bibles where the old stories were changed, where A.J. showed up—have all been gathered up and hidden.

Though Thirty came by the other day to announce that they'd found a previously undiscovered Book of Huldah in some caves outside Jerusalem.

She also said there were a bunch of Shakespeare plays being produced in small theaters around the United States and up in Canada—plays that no one had ever heard of before. Or at least, half the people who went had never heard of them, and the other half insisted they'd known about the plays all their lives.

There was even a sonnet about a wolf who reads love poems to people. Thirty showed it to me before she was called back to Washington.

"You can't just keep leaving people scattered around history like this," she told me. "You—or somebody—is going to have to go back to get them."

I'm not the only one "scattering" them, but Thirty doesn't want to think about that. And anyway, I don't know how she'll be able to use Danger Boy to go after people if I don't have my cap. I was lucky just to get back here.

There is some good news, though: we analyzed the water that Thea brought back from Huldah's pool—though only a few drops survived the journey. But it was enough. They're finding out that some kind of algae grew in that pool, and it coated minerals in the water in such a way that the body could absorb them easier. Things like magnesium and zinc, according to what Thirty was saying.

I don't get it all, but apparently that could help your nervous system while the slow pox was attacking—your body could still send regular messages to itself and keep functioning and not get overwhelmed by the fake nerve-system signals created by the virus.

But that particular kind of algae seems to be extinct, too, so the DARPA people may try to duplicate it in one of their labs, make a kind of vitamin thing for people who catch the kind of slow pox Thea had. The "unauthorized" kind.

Maybe DARPA can do something useful, or at least something that doesn't have to remain a big fat secret and can actually help people.

The DARPA people are studying Thea here, too. Because there's also something in her blood that let her react to the minerals and stuff in the water, that allowed her body to heal, the way some people have certain kinds of antibodies, or the way my body lets me time travel, with the cap. It may help speed the healing or make the recovery more complete, helping them fight a disease that wasn't supposed to still be around.

I have some projects of my own, too. Right now, with the information A.J. gave me, Dad's trying to find out more about Project Split Second and what really happened to my mom back in the '60s. If we can pinpoint her again and if Dad can finally learn to control, and direct, what happens with his time spheres, maybe we can bring her home at last — get to her before Rolf does — and be a family again.

But for now, it's just Dad and Thea and me in the Moonglow. Though Thirty made sure there are still guards outside, to control who gets in — and probably who gets out.

So when Andy comes back with his family, I'll tell them to let him in.

According to the Comnet message I got, I think they'll be here within the hour. His parents were still touring the West, and they were planning on coming back this way.

Plus, it's official business, since his mom is working on slow pox.

I've been checking up on Bible stories, too, since we've been back, and Jeremiah was right. Jerusalem — Israel — was eventually rebuilt. The temple, everything. But then it was destroyed again. And built back. And then invaded again, and fought over, round and round.

Like lots of places in the world.

When Andy and I were little, the only fighting

we worried about was the stuff happening inside our games:

> *Listen: I know we're not as young as we used to be, but do you still play Barnstormers? I do. I'm still making up new characters. Maybe I can show you one, if we ever see each other again. I call him Rubble-Rouser. He's a power hitter, a kind of a Golem/Frankenstein creature, who can smash things to pieces. . . .*

Smashing things to pieces is the easy part. It's putting them back together that's hard.

It's a good day here in the Valley of the Moon. A good day in a crazy world with my friend Thea and my dad.

I see one of the Twenty-Fives sort of twitching in front of the house, reacting to something he hears.

The electric hum of a van engine.

Andy's family.

It will be good to see him again after all this time.

ACKNOWLEDGMENTS

The ongoing caveat remains in force, as it will through the balance of the series: all those previously thanked should consider themselves still thanked, always appreciated. I don't know if it takes a village to write a book, but it sure takes a whole network of kindness, patience, and general good humor.

In that regard, I'd like to thank my sons, Eli and Asher, who let their dad dip into the time stream when he had to, though they'd rather have been playing ball or watching a DVD with him. I'd also like to thank all my splendid editors at Candlewick: Monica Perez, who started this book with me before other vistas called her away; Amy Ehrlich, who jumped right in and did a lot of rereading of earlier books to make sure it all made sense; and Kaylan Adair, who took the reins from Amy when the dust settled and worked hard to make sure that the best possible story, lurking under all those drafts, would emerge.

And given the particular content of this installment in the saga, I'd like to thank all the students I've ever had at Leo Baeck Temple — they've been some of my best teachers. Along with them, I thank the entire bunch of folks I've worked with at Leo Baeck — it's been, and remains, a pleasure. Also, in particular, Rabbis Victor and Nadya Gross and the whole Ohr Hadash group, who originally got my thoughts spinning in the direction that eventually led to these pages.

Eli's adventures continue in
Episode 5

Danger Boy
Fortune's Fool

"What are we doing here?" I ask Shakespeare. "I don't want to see an animal fight."

"Bearbaiting, dogfights, and the mauling of cockerels all make for good sport, young lord," Shakespeare says to me, pulling his felt hat lower on his head. "And even better business."

"People really pay to watch animals kill each other?"

"The Queen's fair citizens enjoy wagering on the outcome. And we welcome the winners next door to the Globe—they spend well on both ha'penny seats and victuals."

"What's a victual?"

"Food, young lord. Grew you in some wild wood, far from the mother tongue?" Shakespeare stares at me like I'm giving him one of Clyne's smiles, with all the extra teeth. "And since we have food and our plays run from afternoon to nearly eventide, those growling stomachs mean a brace of new customers—and more income for the players. Of course, those who lose at wagering come round, too. They find their appetites just as willful. Only, when it comes to the purchase of a ticket, they stand on their legs, instead of digging deeper for a seat."

"They stand? On their feet? Through a whole Shakespeare play!?" I say it without thinking, and he gives me a look that isn't entirely happy.

"Prefer you Marlowe or Johnson's work then?"

I regret this whole conversation right away, for two reasons. The first is that I can't really leave by myself, because of all the pickpockets and crooks who are supposed to be roaming around outside, so I'm stuck here with Shakespeare until this whole disgusting animal massacre thing is over, and talking about it is making it worse. The second is that the talk about growling stomachs reminds me how hungry I am, and pretty much the only kinds of food for sale are big chunks of meat and different kinds of ale, which turns out to be just another word for beer. I already had enough meat for a lifetime when I was with Lewis and Clark and eating buffalos all the time, and I don't feel like getting drunk for the first time ever.

I mean, I don't even know what getting drunk is, really—at least, not firsthand. I've seen some adults do it, though. Like when my dad would have too much wine and start crying about how my mom was gone.

"Good day, young master. Bit o' grog?"

It's a lady with long brown hair and pretty eyes who looks like she's dressed for a Renaissance fair—except, of course, she's not, because we're in the actual Renaissance. I'm the one who's dressed weird. I mean, the fluffy borrowed shirt's an okay disguise, I guess, but I still have my sneakers on. I move my feet under the bench, hoping she won't see them.

"Now, Winifred, it is far too early in the day to corrupt this boy. I fain he keep his wits for the tasks I have at hand."

Even though they're supposed to be speaking English, I'm glad I have the lingo-spot when words like fain pop up in the conversation. The ballpark speaker echo effect kicks in, and as I hear "fain," the lingo-spot lets me know that he simply means "prefer" or "rather."

Why can't he just say that, even if he is Shakespeare?

"Well, 'at's too bad, Will. I'd say this one's a right charmer." She pinches my cheek and I blush, feeling like a little kid, and some part of me—the part that notices how pretty Winifred's eyes are—doesn't want to feel that way and then feels dumb for blushing.

Winifred moves on to the next customers. All the wooden benches are filling up with people— mostly men, but not only; there are lots of women *here, too, and other boys, and even girls — who've come to watch this . . . what? Sport?*

How can it be a sport? The bear is chained to a wall!

"Down there be none but Harry Hunks," Shakespeare says, nodding toward the bear, who shakes his head back and forth, sniffing the air and swatting his paw through it. "Like Winifred, he is a local force of nature. But unlike Winifred, poor old Harry is blind."

"He's blind? That's not fair at all!"

"Unfair? Lad, Harry has sent many a cur to his maker over the years and is scarcely the worse for wear." Shakespeare looks around as if he's sniffing the air just like the bear is. "Yet much as I appreciate the furry old ruffian, we have not come to watch him lord it over his four-legged rivals. We have come for somewhat darker business." He looks around again to make sure no one is watching us, and no one is. Winifred is selling lots of ale, and everyone is ready for the show to begin.

"What darker business?"

"Know you not, with your mysterious arrival in London? I thought you were the very messenger sent by—" Another bearlike sniff of the air. "Well, then, let us say it simply involves those freshly back from the dead, midnight messages, and the belief that words themselves can upend thrones."

It's like I need a dictionary around this guy. But I don't need a dictionary to get the "freshly back from the dead" thing.

"Zombies? Look, Mr. Shakespeare, not that I believe in zombies outside a Barnstormers game, but if what you meant when you said you had something in mind to help put goats in my pocket is something weird, well, maybe I should reconsider. I don't need zombies, and I don't need goats. I need some travel money for food and supplies so I can find my friend Thea, who's disappeared into the forest."

"That does sound like quite the adventure. But I said groats, my good young lord. Groats. Angels and groats."

He can see from my face that I don't know

what he's talking about, but because half of what he says is more or less in recognizable English, the lingo-spot keeps flickering on and off, like a Comsite with a bad sound connection.

"Money," Shakespeare explains, at the same time the lingo-spot kicks in. "What far land did you say you hail from? With such a debased form of Queen's English as your mother tongue?"

But before I can answer, they bring the "dog" `in and there's a big cheer from the crowd. Everyone's clapping and yelling and buying more ale from Winifred.

But this dog looks too big to be a dog.

It actually looks like . . . a picture of that wolf that Thirty showed me. The one that was in the carnival, with Clyne.

Clyne? The Fish Man?

There's a voice in my head. It almost sounds familiar.

Does someone here know the Fish Man? Whose thought was that?

More lingo-spot tingling. Except this time, it's the whole thought-connection thing Clyne was de-

scribing back when we were still stuck in the ruins of old Jerusalem.

Who knows the Fish Man? Or did you know him as the Dragon Man instead? He acquired many names.

It is that wolf! Silver Eye! Or one just like her.

Yes, I am Silver Eye. Who is that?

She's being dragged toward Harry Hunks, the blind bear, but she's looking out over the crowd, trying to find a face.

Trying to find my face.

"We do not usually sport with wolves," Shakespeare says. "This is a rare day indeed!"

Harry is growling. Silver Eye is tied with ropes, and when those are cut and she's released, this crowd expects one of them to die.

What do I do now?